WARLORD

BY

MIRIAM NEWMAN

DCL Publications, LLC

www.thedarkcastlelords.net

First Edition June 2020

DCL Publications
1033 Plymouth Dr.
Grafton, OH 44044

ISBN 978-1-7347690-1-2

This is a work of fiction. Names, characters, places and incidents are the product of the author's imagination, and any resemblance to any actual persons, living or dead, events, or locales, is entirely coincidental.

Cover design by Lynn Hubbard
Cover photo: Can Stock Photo stryjek

PUBLISHED IN THE UNITED STATES OF AMERICA

Chapter One

The birds of death flew overhead. Sharp-eyed hawks and their lesser kin, the kites, were always first to investigate. Later, carrion eaters would come and that was as it should be. There was a double sky burial at the camp of Senec of the Horsetails.

The man for whom the camp now was named sat motionless atop a bay warhorse, framed by innumerable prayer flags straining at red silken cords. More flags than anyone had ever seen flew in honor of Senec's father and his oldest half-brother, Dyak, dead within hours of each other.

He was the only one mounted. Everyone else was afoot, from his father's gray-haired eldest wife to the priests. The visiting dignitaries seemed uncomfortable, but he did not offer to ease their burden, even when priests cast incense into the funeral fire. Not even when a bilious cloud wafted straight into the faces of Westenian representatives. He restrained a smile. Later, he would have to conduct negotiations with those men and with Juragians, too. It would not do to have it said he laughed aloud at the funeral of men he had reputedly murdered.

Made restive by the smoke and flapping sounds from the flags, Senec's mount stamped impatiently. "Be still," he murmured with a gentle chuck at the bit and a hand on the animal's withers. The horse shook his head, resentful of the smoke and the restraint, but Senec only stroked him. The horse was still young, and showed promise. Like men, horses needed a certain mettle for war. His father, Atulfa, had taught him that.

He sighed. The shrunken frame of his aged father barely showed on the funeral bier and soon would be gone. Wind and its minions would accomplish their work despite the fine trappings given as if these were honorable rites. Well, Atulfa had been an honorable man, once.

Veering away from the thought, Senec regarded his father's wives, from the gray-haired old crone who was Dyak's mother to the young girl sent from a mountain kingdom. Most of Atulfa's wives were doddering, but that would not prevent them making minced meat of the girl now that she was without the old man's protection. He would have to move her into his tent before sundown. Another detail. Like his horse, Senec felt a restless stir, a shudder of the spirit. He was also young and longed to be out on a fine warm spring day, hawking or courting a girl like that one. But all he could do was compose his features into a mask of inscrutability.

The priests began chanting, instructing the souls of the departed on making their way to the afterlife. Atulfa, at least, had suspected the journey was near. Dyak, pompous and arrogant until the last, had never considered it even as his body was seized by the rigor of death. They said his half-brother died with a look of surprise upon his face.

* * * *

The funeral rites were interminable. She dared not fidget, but Ganina thought she would broil in her tight, long-sleeved black jacket. She had dressed with special care, prompting Atulfa's older wives to accuse her of already looking for her next husband, and it cost her dearly. Her skirt was loose but belted, and beneath its concealing length she wore heavy black felt boots. She had neither eaten nor drunk for twenty-four hours, since next of kin were required to fast, and the sun beat down upon her. Desperate, she curled her fingers into her palms until her nails cut the skin. If she was taken to the wives' tent, she was as good as dead. She dared not faint.

Abruptly, she felt someone kick her right foot. Startled and wondering if the blows from Atulfa's widows had already begun, she jerked her head up, looking straight into the blue eyes of the Westenian chief. He had to have done it. Her fair cheeks burned as though the wind had blown upon them for hours. She could not pronounce his name, she spoke not a word of his language and they were enemies, but he had just saved her life.

Directly in front of her, the man into whose mercy she might be given sat astride his horse like something carved of stone. Despite the heat, Ganina shivered. Most Covetian men eschewed facial hair, but Senec sported a short brown beard and mustache that helped to conceal his youth. With his hair tied back in the knot of mourning, his hazel eyes seemed more prominent and what Ganina had seen there did not reassure her. He had the look of a killer: cold, pitiless, without remorse. People said his wives had put scorpion juice on the razors of his father and half-brother when Senec's payment to the camp's witches did not bring about their demise. She believed it. Even at rest, his fingers curled around the shaft of a spear attached to his stirrup-holder. Every member of the camp knew they were bound to the authority that spear represented. The time of Atulfa was over.

How would she live, tied to a man like Senec? But she would die if he did not take her. The older wives had hated her from the day she arrived two years before, given by her father to the Warlord. She was pretty and there was always the chance a good-looking young girl could cause the old man's staff to rise again. They had seen what happened when Atulfa made a mid-life marriage with Senec's mother, Lorini. The wives taken as young brides had been relegated to second place, their offspring ignored while the Juragian woman gave birth to child after child. Even Caln, the brat she had brought with her, was tolerated. Though she had finally died in labor with yet another, her first son by Atulfa was now their leader. There had been no escape from her influence.

Lorini was beyond their reach, but Ganina was not.

"Whore." The nearly inaudible voice reached Ganina like

a ghostly specter, more frightening than any that might rise from a bier. It was Odeena, Dyak's mother. "Count your remaining hours."

Hers was no idle threat. The wives might be older, but they had the strength of little oxen and there were a lot of them. In two years, they had cracked Ganina's ribs and bruised her regularly, though they had to stop short of marring her beauty. That would have angered Atulfa, who liked to look at her since there was nothing else he could do to her.

Without him, they would fall upon her that night, beating the soles of her feet until she couldn't stand to defend herself. Then they would finish the job with stones and drag her into the brush to be eaten by wild dogs. It had happened to widows before.

She had lived in a torment of fear from the moment Atulfa died. It was wearing her down. Even if Senec took her—and she had no assurance he would—that meant living with two hostile older wives, presumptive murderesses. It did not represent a great improvement.

Desperately, she glanced aside at the Westenian whose name she couldn't say. But some things did not need words. There would be a funeral feast in Atulfa's great red-dyed tent, at which his widows would serve the guests as a mark of respect. The foreign chief would be there. She must get close enough to tempt him. If he took her for the night and she pleased him, perhaps she would be given to him. Anything to leave the dreadful camp that had been her waking nightmare for two years.

He wasn't bad-looking: tall, blond, bearded. It could be worse. She had never known a man; Atulfa had been too old and disabled to take another wife in anything but name. The thought of lying with one terrified her, but it was that or death. Seen in that light, he was really quite attractive.

Chapter Two

Its thin-worn walls bulged with air currents, but Atulfa's tent was floored with priceless carpets. The dining dais was set with fine bone utensils, kiln-fired plates and silver goblets. Vases of purple and white mountain asters adorned the middle and at every place there were bowls of warm water with flower petals floating in them. Outside, meat that had come from the hunting and trapping of old men and boys roasted over precious firewood while the rest of the tribe made do with peat.

Atulfa had taught his sons that public occasions were the time to exhibit wealth and power. Of course, even Senec's camp had none now except for mysterious gold coin he seemed able to produce at will, but that was enough. No one else had anything at all. By the end of the war with Westenia, Covetians had been reduced to eating dogs and rats, roots and moldy grain. Ganina could feel her mouth water and her stomach clench at smells coming from the outdoor kitchens.

"Slut!" Atulfa's third wife spat, cuffing her on the way in. But Ganina had no recourse. Those whose language she spoke did not care if she was abused, and those who might care did not share her tongue.

"Look sharp, there, girl," Breaca growled, striking Ganina

knuckles-first across the back of the skull, so she hurried to the head of the ring of half-reclining men, with a platter of roast rabbit. Others wives were kneeling, pouring chica, offering loaves of new bread and sweet butter. There were platters of roasted wild onions and carrots, tureens of mashed peas flavored with pepper and garlic, small birds roasted whole and drizzled with honey. None of the women would be allowed to take food until the men were fed. Ganina gritted her teeth, willing them to hurry, keeping her expression neutral as they made their choices. None of them hurried.

There was a sudden breath of welcome air as the tent flap lifted. Senec and his counselors had arrived. All of his advisers were Covetians, smaller men than Senec, who showed his mother's Juragian blood. Though he had his father's dark skin, his hair had bleached lighter than that of the tribesmen and his eyes were hazel and elongated like his mother Lorini's. Burnished muscle showed beneath the short sleeves of his hot-weather tunic; what he lacked in height compared to the foreigners, he made up for in brute strength. Ganina shuddered, imagining his hands on her. Who knew what really passed between a man and woman in the privacy of their sleeping quarters? His children did not fear him, but everyone else did.

"My honored guests!" Senec exclaimed in Covetian, while translators murmured to the Juragian and Westenian. Everyone knew Senec spoke his mother's Juragian tongue yet oddly, that day, he did not choose to do so. "This is a sad occasion, but our hearts are gladdened that you share it with us. Accept my thanks."

"It was on my way," the Westenian said, in his own language, but Ganina saw her leader's eyes light with an unmistakable spark of laughter before the translator spoke. She supposed Senec might have learned some Westenian from his half-brother, Caln. Roundly rejected by Atulfa's tribe, Caln had gone to Westenia the moment his mother died. It was under Covetian control then. He had fought Senec when the Westenians rose in rebellion, even supplying his new land with lightning fire that devastated his former homeland. Yet, incredibly, he and Senec remained close. People thought he had given Senec gold. Ganina supposed enough gold could buy redemption.

What surprised her was that Senec was amused. There was a small undercurrent of laughter at the dais, from everyone but the Juragian, who looked as though he had a large stick jammed up his ass.

Senec carefully rinsed his hands, and then—to her horror—looked straight at Ganina. "Attend us." His tone was unthreatening; even so, she had to force her feet to the task. Yet since she carried a quantity of roast rabbit in savory juice, it stood to reason that she should serve the newly-arrived men. She had just begun to do so, starting with Senec, when he stilled her by trapping her wrist. It was not a harsh touch, but she stopped immediately.

"Your hands are cold, Ganina," he said. "You should eat."

He snapped his fingers in the general direction of Breaca. "Serve her," he said and then, to the stupefaction of everyone in the tent, patted the place beside him and moved his legs aside. "Come, sit."

There was silence in which the only sound was of the spoon in old Breaca's hand knocking against the wooden dish as she ladled out meat. Ganina was equally petrified, yet Senec's presence beside her guaranteed safety. He had just staked his claim. He would not make her his whore since her father controlled many men on the border with Juragia. No, her fate as Senec's wife was sealed. Across the dais, the Westenian had no expression. Why should he? She belonged to another man now.

Unexpectedly, anger bloomed in her gut—in part, bitter disappointment at being unable now to escape the camp. There was the frustration of knowing she would never learn if she might have wanted that blond chieftain; she thought she could have. Above all, it was rage at having been simply possessed, yet again, like a horse or cow. Her father had given her to Atulfa; now Senec had taken her. Always, she was in the power of men. And why? Only because they were larger and stronger. She thought of Senec's wives. Had they felt the heady sensation of vengeance, seeking the deaths of Atulfa and Dyak? How many years had they waited?

When Senec held a morsel of rabbit to her lips, she took it.

Despite her hunger, it tasted like ashes. But he had decided to dote on her, apparently. He buttered bread and passed it to her, a service never given by a man to a woman. Ganina silently filled his goblet and then her own with cool water because Senec was not known for taking hard drink. Perhaps at the end of the meal he might have a little mead, but that would be all. No one had ever seen him drunk, unlike his father whose drinking bouts were legendary.

He continued conversing with Torm of the Twin Rocks, a Warlord greatly reduced in stature as all the Lords were, but still shrewd and influential.

"It is a tragedy," Senec said blandly, "yet my father was no longer of an age to deal with drawn-out negotiations, nor of a temperament for it."

No one could dispute that. Atulfa's rages were the stuff of legends. When Senec had returned from Westenia—taken prisoner there but released through Caln's good offices—his father had promised to have his brothers cut off his balls because Senec proposed a treaty with a country that had blasted them to bits with lightning fire. Atulfa's people had prayed for peace before all of them perished, but the old man was prepared to lose every man, woman and child to appease his pride. Even after he had been forced to sue for peace, everyone had known it was only a matter of time before he plunged his people back into war. He cared nothing for their suffering.

Was that why Senec had killed him? Ganina had simply assumed he wanted to be Warlord. Dyak would have done exactly as his father had, but now that both men were dead, the people had peace. She rolled the thought around in her mind, gnawing it like a bone.

"Fortunately, our ice houses in the north kept our honored ones until Lord Ifelsten could stop by...on his way." Senec favored the Westenian with an ironic stare. "We were more fortunate in Lord Lembach's proximity. He was already here. I felt it best to have the bodies preserved so that our...allies...could be assured of whom we were consecrating."

"Wise," the Juragian envoy said, and then drank more wine. He should be getting drunk; his goblet had been refilled several times. Ganina thought all the men save Senec were feeling their liquor. No one was paying her the slightest attention, so she helped herself to honey-drenched squab. It appeared she could eat what she liked, so she did, growing increasingly interested in the conversation, even if it was through interpreters. Women rarely heard these things. They only lived with the results.

"My father and brother even now find the path to bliss," Senec said piously, "and in the morning we may speak of other things."

"Or we may not."

The Juragian was not drunk after all; it appeared he was refusing negotiations. But why? His land had not participated in the recent war. Did he feel there was nothing to negotiate? In that case, why was he at their camp?

"Suit yourself," Ifelsten said, and belched.

Senec turned to him with a hint of a smile, signaling the translator that he wished to speak. "I propose we see my horse herd in the morning. You are noted for your horsemanship. These animals are of old and honored breeding."

"Yes, I know," Ifelsten replied. "I would be delighted." He rinsed his hands as though finished with something, though desert had not been served.

"Coming, Lembach?" Senec inquired of the Juragian, while translators chattered busily. He still had not seen fit to converse with his mother's countryman in her tongue. But her family had cut ties with her when she married a Covetian. Perhaps Senec had no use for their language—or anything else.

"I am sure they are very fine," the envoy said tonelessly. "No doubt my business can wait until you have exhibited them." Ganina raised her head ever-so-slightly. It was the first crack in Lembach's stony façade. He did want something.

The women were bringing in precious ices from the northern mountains...Ganina's home. She jumped despite herself when Breaca set one down in front of her so heavily that some of the concoction sprayed on her black jacket. Immediately Senec's headman, Donleth, appeared as if by magic.

"You need rest, old woman," he said, grasping her elbow

with more force than compassion. "Come and I will give it to you."

The venerable warrior was entirely capable of meaning eternal rest. Breaca paled and sagged, but Donleth was a veteran of many battles, still strong despite his age. Giving her a jolt that would have started a horse, he hauled her out of the tent while Senec looked on, unspeaking. When she was gone, the Warlord reached to flick the damage off Ganina's jacket. She sat, as trapped as one of those rabbits she had just eaten, as his fingers lightly stroked the curve of her collar bone beneath the material.

"She has stained your jacket."

"It's all right," she managed to choke. "I have more."

Senec caressed her briefly, his intention crystal clear. Ganina could actually feel her pulse pounding where he was touching her. Oddly, she found herself desiring the touch although she knew it was only a matter of sating his lust. Still, no one had ever handled her as if she mattered and, for that moment, it felt good.

Chapter Three

Finally, Senec could get the image of those platforms out of his mind. He nodded at one of the wives, indicating he would accept mead. Its honeyed warmth slid down his throat like a blessing, obliterating a small measure of tension, though he dared not enjoy too much of it. His enemies would find him no drunken fool, and though peace had been declared between their countries and a compact signed, not one of them doubted they were still enemies.

It was too bad, he thought. He could have liked Ifelsten and had marked that the Westenian paid Ganina closer attention than was necessary. Might he find more profit in the end from giving her to a man who wanted her rather than taking her for himself?

He looked sidelong at the girl sitting obediently in the place he had given her. Her father was a man with a large following, but the girl represented riches of a different sort. Women of the southern tribes suffered by comparison. Dark as half-baked dough to shield them from relentless sun, with round brown eyes that saw well in darkness and spare frames ideally suited to a hard land, they had never appealed to him. There was much of his mother in Senec and the reddish hair, fair skin and clear gray eyes of his father's youngest widow drew him.

She could not be more than twenty. Her hair was gracefully coiffed; her neck was a marble column below a perfectly symmetrical oval face. She had a broad brow, wide set intelligent eyes and a mouth made for kissing. One could have dressed her in a sack and the fine lines of her body would still have been visible. Though the women had done their best to make her cower, Ganina still bore herself with pride that would distinguish his house. He felt a pleasant stirring of the loins each time he looked at her...too pleasant to give her away.

"You will move your things to my tent this night," he told her in a low voice. "Men will accompany you to ensure your safety." To ensure that she didn't run, as well, though he didn't really expect it. After all, he had done very well by her. Few women would have been permitted a seat at a gathering of tribesmen and guests, and when Breaca was forced to pour mead for her, the younger woman's triumph was complete. It was a gift. A wedding gift.

* * * *

The feasting went on for hours and eventually Ganina felt the need to relieve herself.

"My Lord, I must go," she said for his ears alone.

"You may. Donleth will accompany you." He gestured for his father's headman, now his, who stood at the tent flap.

Ganina knew that she was under guard, but it worked two ways. While Donleth guarded her, he also protected her from anything the wives might have planned. She knew him well, so she felt no hesitation accepting his company. Unlike so many, he had never done her the slightest discourtesy.

Still, she halted just outside the flap, disconcerted. There, in full view of those not in the tent—which was nearly everyone—Senec's wives were clambering aboard wagons loaded to the gunnels. Their five daughters accompanied them, weeping bitterly, while the younger wife's three-year-old son screamed in the arms of a nursemaid standing in the dust. A fortune in furnishings and supplies rode in the wagons and Ganina saw that each vehemently protesting woman bore a Warlord's red-and-yellow silk purse wrapped and tied to her belted skirt. The purses were heavy, banging against Illinea's and Drusa's hips. Yet Drusa's greatest treasure was being left behind—her son, Gilya. She had to be hauled bodily aboard the wagon by two strong men.

It was shockingly, painfully obvious that Senec had just divorced the wives who had done his bidding and was returning them to their homes along with their female children. He would not give up his son, of course. The women were accompanied by great riches and their dowries were intact, so their fathers would be mollified. But how did you separate a mother from her child? Ganina considered them both evil women, yet she looked aside in pity.

It was all the more unexpected, then, to have the oldest wife's wrath descend on her.

"Whore! Infidel!" Illinea shrieked, pointing a bony, shaking finger at her. "It is for you we are cast out. It is for you Drusa's son is abandoned! You will rue this day! I promise it!"

Ganina looked back, horrified, with an unstudied "Who, me?" expression for all the camp to see.

"I have done nothing!" she defended herself, and to her surprise Donleth took her arm beneath the elbow, gesturing rudely toward the wagons with his free hand.

"You brought it upon yourselves," he admonished both women. "Now go."

The drivers clucked; the women and children screamed. It was pandemonium as dust clouds jetted up from the protesting wheels of the heavily-burdened wagons, which began their long journey with renewed wails from both departing wives. Drusa's son screamed and sobbed so pitifully that Ganina sped to the privies, sure that she would be sick. She wasn't, but it was a long time before she emerged.

"You will be a woman of importance now," Donleth said. "Accustom yourself to bearing the envy and spite of others. It is part of what made Illinea what she is."

Ganina felt surprise, wondering if the taciturn headman had harbored feelings for Senec's wife. She had never seen any sign of it, but she knew the warriors kept their tender emotions close. Usually those were exhibited only to their children, and even that was rare. Atulfa had roundly abused his offspring to his dying day.

"Come," Donleth said, breaking her trance. "The sun sets low and we must move your belongings. I can protect you from the women, but not their tongues. Prepare yourself."

Startled, Ganina noted the angle of the sun…the ochre-brown and light purple streaks beginning to inch across the sky. Darkness fell speedily on the plains of Covetia and pinpoints of light would soon appear, the gods' gift of stars. They might have been the last things she had ever seen. Now, because Senec wanted her, she had a chance at life, so she followed Donleth without a word. She would have preferred to go to the blond chief and left the dreadful camp behind, but a woman must take her fate as it came. So she walked with Donleth along the pony lines, where he nodded at a small boy who untied two sturdy mounts, falling in behind them. Her business was known.

The headman had been correct. As they passed, a line of flinty-eyed women gathered, their smoke-stained skirts gripped by children whose frightened faces peeked out from folds of material. At first they were silent, but as she neared the tent of the wives finally one of them spoke, as if afraid Ganina might escape into its depths without proper chastisement.

"They are cast out for YOU, foreigner!" Ganina could not see the speaker, safely shielded by ranks of tribeswomen. "We have seen you parade yourself for Senec, with your husband still living. For shame, harlot!"

"No!" Ganina began to protest, but Donleth shook his head at her, sternly.

"They will not listen. Save your breath."

He gave the women a look of open threat. "Let any stone fly and we will stake you out naked in the desert this night, to give the dogs and jackals your complaint."

"Would you ruin the tribe entirely?" one demanded. "Our men are already dead!"

The headman gave a quiet, "Hunh." To the woman, he said only, "We can get more of you."

"They did Senec's will!" another complained.

"Go back to your tents," Donleth ordered. "NOW!"

They went, muttering sullenly, and since never at any time had Donleth paused in his stride or permitted her to do so, Ganina went into the tent which had been her unhappy home. It was a sturdier shelter than Atulfa's. An unused cook fire ringed by stones sat in the middle of the floor. The rugs were of reed finely bound with strong thread and the wives' beds hugged the circumference of the tent, separated by strings of brightly colored wooden beads that formed curtains. Their beds were covered with woolen blankets woven in broad bands of gay colors. Dresses, shawls and fans lay strewn across some, while others were bare and neat.

Ganina's was one of the neat beds. She retrieved her sandals from beneath it and her boots and gowns and skirts and jackets from carved wooden chests on either side of the bed. There were the few toiletries she used, some jewelry Atulfa had given her, and a fan for hot weather…the sum total of two years. They did not even have to use the second pony, who sniffed eagerly for shoots of grass in the shade of the tent while his less fortunate partner was loaded.

When the paltry burden had been wrapped in lengths of cotton, secured by cord and strapped on, Donleth led the patient animal a short distance to Senec's purple tent from which his wives had just been expelled. He lifted the flap and Ganina went into her new home. It had been stripped bare. Not a rug was there, not a child's toy or a blanket, not a mug or plate. His spiteful wives had taken every item and apparently Senec had let them. It would have been easy to have stopped them, but he hadn't bothered. Only his large bed, covered in rich brocades, remained. Donleth placed her possessions upon it, having nowhere else to put them except in the dirt, bowed to her briefly and left. Apparently, her presence was no longer required at the banquet, which she knew might still go on for several hours or all night. She had no way of knowing if Senec would come or when. She was alone.

Chapter Four

Well after the gibbous moon was up, she heard a scuffling outside and the tent flap parted, revealing Donleth and the pony boy. Apparently, there were no other men to spare, because they bore a hammered copper tub used by the most privileged for bathing. Ganina watched them place it against one side of the tent and summon additional boys. A ragged speechless line of youngsters entered, some staggering under the weight of cauldrons. They were the same little boys who had stolen squab on the plains that afternoon to feed their guests and carried grime in with them, looking more in need of a bath than she. Ganina had bathed at the river that morning before the funeral rites, but those little ones looked like water never touched them. They did their work silently and departed.

Donleth did not speak, either, just put down a jar of soap, drying cloths and some mats, bowing briefly before departing. He had never bowed to her when she was Atulfa's wife, but she would be Senec's on the morrow. He would take her to the priests to have their wrists ritually bound with red silk while the words of joining were pronounced, then return with her to the tent for three days of unbridled sex. When she emerged, she would be a woman, bedded and bound like all the rest while the camp waited to see if his seed would blossom inside her. No one would be satisfied until it did and she could depend upon his undivided attention until that time. Some women had suffered their husbands' nightly attentions for a year before conceiving. She shivered.

Sounds of revelry still came from the red tent, so she slipped gratefully out of her sweat-stained clothes and into the tub. The privilege was rare, so no matter her trepidation about the night to come, she could not resist. Reaching behind her, she took down the long, copper-colored hair that set her apart from every woman in that camp. It was not unusual in the north, where Covetians had intermarried with lighter-complexioned Juragians for many generations, but in Atulfa's camp it was the badge which had earned her the title of foreigner.

Still, she knew men admired it. Senec would, so she left it down. If she had been a young virgin and this the night before their wedding, she would have slept in the tent with the other women, giggling or being comforted into the late hours of darkness. But she was no longer young and technically presumed not to be a virgin. So Senec could have her when he wished and, judging by his behavior at the banquet, he wished it to be that night.

She sponged and rinsed carefully with rare sea sponges brought all the way through Westenia, then considered what to do about her hair. It was sweaty and she longed to wash it, but it took hours to dry. On the other hand, celebrations such as she had left often went on nearly until dawn. She doubted she would be able to sleep, but if there was any chance at all she knew she would be more comfortable with her hair washed. So she coiled its silky masses into the tub, bending gracefully to lather it with a gob of the gelatinous concoction of lanolin and soap root.

Refreshed, she stepped reluctantly from the tub at last onto reed mats people favored in warmer weather and then into silk slippers. Her wardrobe had not required much seductive sleepwear, but she did have a sheer linen gown she knew showed every line of her body. Donning it, she spent a good half hour working snarls out of her hair with a wooden comb, then scented her tresses with lavender. There was still no sign of Senec. Well, the gods knew when he would come, she thought, and it was growing cooler. Aware that her skin was prickling in goosebumps, she slid under the brocade coverlet and crisp cotton sheet. The bed had been ringed with rosemary to repel insects; its woody scent filled her nostrils for a long time before sleep came.

Senec entered so quietly, she knew he was there only by the glow of the single oil lamp he carried. Her eyes flew open. She thought it was very late; she caught the faintest glimpse of dead-dark night spangled with stars and then the flap dropped behind him and he was in the tent with her. She lay still, feigning sleep, but she had faced the opening and by the light of that one lamp she could see him as he set it on the floor and undressed. Lowering her lashes just enough that he would not see the whites of her eyes, she watched.

He had dressed well for the rites, in soft suede boots into which he had tucked his best linen dress trousers. Bending, he pulled off the boots, then stood again to unlace the leather jerkin he always wore over a short-sleeved, padded tunic of purple and gold. The tunic went next and he stood before her unsuspected regard, naked to the waist. His skin was tawny gold in the lamplight, with dark nipples on a broad, deep, powerful chest. Most Covetian men had little body hair, but Senec was not all Covetian, and Ganina saw that his chest was lightly marked by brown hair denoting northern blood, a bloodline they shared.

It was not all they would share that night. He stripped off his linen trousers and the loincloth beneath and she saw Senec naked for the first time. Ganina swallowed nervously, praying he could not hear. A tan line stopped just above his buttocks, leaving an incongruous space of white backside, but it was not that which concerned her. Below his taut belly, amidst more of that surprisingly light hair, her soon-to-be husband had a very respectable male endowment. His legs were powerful, well muscled from a lifetime of physical activity. There would be no escape from the demands of his body. He was a warrior, a man used to taking what he wanted. Ganina felt her mouth dry up with fear while her insides seemed to quake.

He left the oil lamp on, surprising her. His lifting of the covers was not a surprise, nor his quietly spoken, "Ganina."

She opened her eyes.

"I didn't want to frighten you."

"I wasn't frightened," she lied. It felt like something was clutching her throat with choking hands. Senec studied her by lamplight.

"You are very beautiful," he said softly.

She couldn't answer.

"Did my father touch you? As a husband?"

She just shook her head.

"Did you take a lover?"

If he believed that, the danger was incalculable. "My Lord, no!"

"You were wed but never bedded," he pointed out. "An awkward state for a young woman. Tell me truthfully, did you seek a man? I will forgive you one, if so, but tell me now."

"I did not!" she said vehemently. "Your women call me a slut, but I never was. Never!"

To her surprise, Senec smiled. Only a fleeting smile, but unmistakable. He reached to place one finger beneath her chin, lifting it so that she would face him, willing or not. "I will know if you are lying."

"I am not lying."

"All right."

She closed her eyes, feeling his weight as he got into the bed beside her.

Chapter Five

Ganina had not shared a bed since childhood and just the fact that she felt him sink the mattress alarmed her, accentuating as it did his greater size and strength. The day had been a triumph for Senec; he was freed of his father's control, his half-brother's enmity and his shrewish wives. She expected him to put the final tally to his sheet, but to her surprise he only pulled two pillows under his head and shoulders, resting his head against his upper arm. The light cast a miniscule nimbus, lending an intimacy to the occasion that she did not want. It made him seem somehow less threatening, which surely was an illusion.

"Did you bathe?" he inquired amiably.

"Yes. Did you have the bath sent?"

"Yes."

"Thank you." In the course of two years, Ganina had exchanged perhaps a hundred words with Senec. She really had no idea who he was. "It was a great pleasure."

"I do not think you had many pleasures in the tent of the wives."

No, she had always feared a scorpion in her shoe or a blade in her back. She wondered suddenly if Senec entertained the same fear. How would it be for a man, sleeping with women who had done murder? Was that why he had sent them away? He seemed fond of his little daughters. Had it not pained him to part with them? But there was no sign of grief in his face. There was no sign of anything, not even desire. She had no idea what he was thinking.

"It was difficult," she admitted, remembering. She had found ways to cope. After some unpleasant groping, Atulfa had treated her like a bauble to be admired. She had been so meek that she escaped the majority of his rages. Gnarled and bent by the claws of old age, he had been in pain much of the time, and she thought that had not helped. He had died very swiftly. It was a merciful end to his pain, at least.

"I can imagine," Senec replied, reaching out to stroke wisps of drying hair back from the side of her face. She flinched and he paused.

"I am only inexperienced," she said quickly. "I will try to please you, My Lord."

He resumed his touch, studying her body through the thin gown. "You already do." Cupping his hand over the top of her shoulder, he slid one finger beneath the strap of her gown. Slowly, he slipped it down so that her breast was revealed. Ganina drew a quaking breath.

"Exquisite," he said, fondling her. His hands were callused from the work of war and he touched her very gently, as if aware of it, lowering the other strap so that he could cup her other breast, as well. Now he showed desire; his eyes were dark and intent with it. He stroked her until she shifted, disturbed. She knew what she was feeling was desire. But how could she desire a man she barely knew who had simply taken ownership of her? When they had first brought her to that camp, she had been so resentful the men had taken the precaution of binding her wrists. Now she was resigned to her fate, but she had never dreamed it would be Senec. She wanted to hate him, but she craved his touch…anyone's touch. For two years, she had been dead inside. Now, her body was coming to life.

Slowly, he inched closer until she could feel his warmth and smell the pleasantly musky odor of a man who had bathed. He, too, had been to the river.

"You are still young, Ganina," he said. "Wasted until now. You need a man."

Bending, he kissed her breast and she gasped. She was afraid to touch him. His arousal was very near her hip, frightening yet enticing. Until that moment, she had been like a dog that was fed and then forgotten. Atulfa had accepted her because it would have been an insult to her father not to have done so. On public occasions, he exhibited her dressed in finery, to prove he could still be given a young and attractive wife. But no one in that camp had ever wanted her. Except—apparently—Senec. At the thought, she lost her private battle and curled both hands around the back of his head, elbows on his shoulders. His hair was rough and blunt-cut, different from hers. She held it as he slowly kissed her body, tonguing over her collarbone as she remembered his caress there that afternoon. This was what he had wanted to do, even then. And she had wanted it, too.

"You are mine now," he murmured, his breath brushing her skin. "Are you sorry?"

"No," she answered truthfully. His touch was surprisingly delicious. She shifted closer, indicating her acceptance, and felt his erection hard against her body. It excited her in a way nothing had ever done.

Cradling her face in both hands, he took her in a deep, passionate kiss. Though she had never been kissed, she reacted instinctively, parting her lips to give him entry. He tasted of mead and invaded in a slow, leisurely process—toying with her. She moaned low in her throat, arching her body against his. Reassured by his gradual possession, she wanted the touch of his skin on hers then and rubbed her palms in slow circles over his body. He was warm and strong—a young and virile man. Aroused, he shuddered, and she did it again. It was so easy to make a man want you. There was power in it; she could feel it.

He raised himself, pulling her gown down over her hips and feet, throwing it carelessly into the darkness. His hard knee nudged the tender flesh of her thighs and she opened them at once, letting him kneel inside the cradle they made.

He smiled down at her and she knew her obedience

pleased him. Her life depended upon that obedience, yet now she thought perhaps it would not be so difficult. He didn't frighten her as much as she had anticipated.

"You are ready, are you not?" She nodded and he carefully lowered himself onto her. She knew then that he wouldn't harm her. There would be no brutal rape. Though his look was that of a man hunting prey or an enemy—focused, fierce—he did not assault her, only letting her feel the hard press of his erection. He moved against her tender flesh, beginning to ease into her, and she tensed. This would make her a woman, bound to their society and his pleasures.

He pressed her flat with his hips and slowly entered her.

"You did not lie to me," he said, beginning to move forward inexorably. His expression was a mixture of satisfaction, lust and triumph. "You are an honorable woman." In the next moment, he took that honor. She gave a deep grunt of pain and he paused, pulling her face against his, forehead to forehead. She hooked her hands over his shoulders, aware of her own helplessness. It hurt and there was no escaping it.

"Put your legs around me," he instructed. "It will ease you."

Anxious for any relief, she did as he asked and felt him slide into her—shockingly deep. Slowly, he began to move. Her incoherent sounds carried on the wind and though she realized they would be audible to the men standing guard at a distance, she couldn't stop.

On and on it went, steady and relentless, to the accompaniment of Senec's murmured praise and then his soft groans of fulfillment. At first it was a deep, burning pain and Ganina lifted her hips, trying to escape. It only drove him deeper and seemed to ignite something in him. His initial gentleness ebbed, replaced by a driving rhythm so that she could hear the sound of their bodies meeting. Eventually she could only give herself up to it and, as she did, the pain lessened. Senec claimed her then in a hot, passionate kiss, groaning her name. Instinctively, she knew what was coming. He would release his seed very soon, and she wanted it—wanted the hot tide of his life flooding into her, promising a child. When he gave her a child, she would have something to love.

Thinking it, she drove against him in time with his thrusts. Her body settled into a rhythm as old as life itself, her legs locking around him, and his gasp of pleasure told her she was doing it correctly. She felt him begin to shake, straining against her as he reached his climax. Ganina felt no such pleasure, but neither did she feel pain, just a peaking urgency. Then thought left altogether as Senec collapsed on her, nearly rendering her insensible.

She came to herself again amidst a tangle of sheets. The oil lamp had gone out and no hint of dawn yet showed through the heavy tent hides, but she felt Senec sprawled over her and his seed leaking hotly down her thighs. She grimaced, glad that the men had not yet removed her bathing tub. Other than the messiness, she thought, it was not so bad.

Senec stirred and withdrew, rolling onto his side. She winced, feeling strangely empty...hollowed inside. Oddly, she longed to have him back, but he seemed unconscious. After a few minutes, though, she could see the betraying glow of his eyes as he opened them. He put up a lazy hand to caress her hair as he had done before but this time she leaned into his palm.

He was already growing hard again. Without asking, she rose and dipped a sponge into the cooling water of the tub, carrying it back with her. Senec rolled onto his back and lay unmoving and unspeaking as she pressed the sponge to his body, caring for him. He was warm and solid, not a dream that would pass away with the morning, but a living, breathing man who desired her and would come to her time and again when need drove him. She felt his penis stiff and throbbing in her hand and smiled. Yes, she did have power in that camp, after all.

"We will go the priests in the morning," he said. "After that, I am taking Ifelsten to see the horse herd on the border lands. I will gift him, and barter for coal. The Westenians have it in abundance but they are short of grazing lands. With coal we can heat our tents and shoe our horses and forge things we have never had."

Ganina remembered the blond chieftain then, but in a daze that precluded clear thinking. Only Senec claimed her attention at that moment. He would be her husband—not a well-known quantity, to be sure, but not an old man.

"You will not stay with me?" she asked in surprise, but she also put her hand on his chest, stroking him to soften her words.

"You are not a young bride," Senec pointed out, "though we know the truth of it, between us. It would be acceptable for you to come with me. Would you like to ride to the herd lands?"

It would be the greatest freedom she had known in two long years and Ganina's heart leapt up in sheer joy. "Oh, yes!"

"Then you may come," he said, linking his hands with hers and pulling her onto the bed. He kneed her legs apart so that she straddled him. "But ride me first." There was a smile in his voice and she didn't resist, bending to kiss him, taunting and teasing instinctively. It was true that you knew things about a man after sharing his bed, as though the gods had given you a doorway into his mind even though he thought he was the one doing the claiming. She sensed things now about Senec—deep and secret things, of which conversation in the red tent had given her the merest hint. She would learn his ways, make him less a stranger, and hopefully bear him a child. If she could do those things, she had a future.

Chapter Six

The morning dawned fair and clear, though high wispy clouds indicated to Senec's experienced eye that there would be rain later. By then, he would be back in his tent with his bride, so he paid no heed, strolling through dew-covered grass to the pony lines. A good-looking black gelding rolled an eye at him, as if asking whether he would really disturb their rest so early. In fact, Covetian ponies were some of the finest and toughest in the world, suitable for the kind of ride he envisioned that day. But the larger horses they were going to see were finer yet.

He would be able to ride. Senec's head did not pain him, though others would be suffering. The Juragian should have a thunderous hangover and Ifelsten might not arise early. For the first time in many days, Senec had time to be alone with his thoughts, not that they were always good company.

It had been a wise choice, keeping Ganina. She was the tonic he needed, now that her fear of him was lessened. He knew most people did fear him and was not displeased by the fact. It had protected him—oldest son of a Juragian woman, prey for the offspring of Atulfa's Covetian wives. In his youth, Atulfa had been known to strike men dead for insolence or dereliction of duty and no one was quite sure how much of the father was in his son, since they seemed much alike in some ways. Senec was not sure, either.

He hoped he was a better man than his father, but killing your kin was a heavy burden and even if he was never judged by men, he would not escape the judgment of the gods. Abandoning your children...it required no action on the part of the gods to make him suffer for that. The sweetness of his daughters had been the only gentle thing in his life.

But Ganina was a gentle creature, as well, so hungry for any small kindness that he thought even the crumbs he threw her would suffice. He had not given his inner being to any woman since the first days of his passion for Illinea, but Ganina should prove suitable. It would be no chore to bed her and she could give him more children, perhaps some daughters. She might have the status of only wife for a long while, too. He was in no hurry for more...not this time.

Almost against his will, he remembered the image of her atop him, her beautiful body arched over his hands, head thrown back. The girl exuded sensuality despite her best efforts at suppressing it. It was why the other women had hated her, why men had stared at her so that he had suspected her of taking a lover. Once initiated, she had taken him not as a shy young wife, but like a high-priced whore. A woman like that could be dangerous in a much different way than his wives had been. He would have to be careful that he did not become infatuated.

Already he ached with the thought that he could have her again, at his pleasure.

He would have to be careful of Ifelsten, too. The Westenian wanted her and though Senec thought the chief would not overstep the bounds of hospitality, when they had offered him a girl the past night, he had refused. Senec could not think of many nights in Westenia when Ifelsten had not kept one in his bed. He was unmarried and women had fought for the honor, so he was accustomed to having whomever he wanted. It was a hard habit to break.

By then, Senec had reached the bottom of the short hill where Aben the pony boy was on duty, sloe-eyed with sleepiness. But he rose at once when the Warlord gestured.

"Bring two ponies," Senec told him. "The black gelding and another. Put on their best saddles and bridles, with red cloth for decoration." It was the accustomed thing for bridal parties. His practiced gaze assessed the ponies, but the boy had been attentive to their needs. They were shiny from the curry brush, with manes and tails carefully combed out and their hooves darkened by oil. "Have them at my tent in half of an hour."

Ganina had not been negligent, either, and it pleased him to know that she would be ready. She had proved no slug-a-bed even after vigorous lovemaking, but had risen and summoned men to remove the bath and then swept out the tent behind them. Donleth had brought them bread and meat and watered wine to break fast, and then Ganina had laid out clothes for both of them, selecting for Senec from among an armful his headman brought from the-gods-knew-where. His wives had even taken his clothing. But he sensed he now had a woman who would keep good order in his tent and camp. That had been Drusa's job, which she had neglected. The only thing she had given him aside from several months of lust was his son, Gilya, conceived in a first excess of passion. The child had slept with his nursemaid since losing his mother, but Senec knew he would have to go to see Gilya. First, there was the matter of marriage.

* * * *

"You have lost no time in taking another bride, I see." Jaric's ironic tone cut deeply, but Senec could not retaliate against a priest. At least, not presently. He would need the support of the priests in coming days and months.

"The women would have killed her," he pointed out.

"Killing seems not to disturb you that much." His sharp-eyed elder priest looked him up and down, not in a flattering way. Though Jaric might privately admit the need to dispatch men who brought dishonor and death to the tribe, putting away wives with small children was a different matter. Even if those women had killed Atulfa and Dyak, unacknowledged guilt lay on Senec's head and he knew he would have trouble with the priest on that account.

"One does not execute wives without proof of murder," he reminded the man. He had been very careful to see there was no proof, but Senec maintained the self-serving fiction begun the moment those men were dead. "Yet I cannot have that taint in our camp. Can you think I do not grieve for my children, whom I sent away as well? But it is the price of this thing."

The older man gave him a look of distaste no one else would have dared. "Your father sold the honor of our camp and the bones of twenty-four noble sons for the sake of easy takings. Not so easy, were they? Now you treat with his enemies. I do not envy you that task or any other you have done." Then he shrugged. "Very well, bring the girl in and I will bind you."

It was over quickly, with only a second priest present as a witness. Senec noted that Ganina had gowned herself properly in a gray gown with a red sash—red for celebration, but the plainest of dress because she was a widow. Her discretion pleased him. They returned to their ponies and Donleth parted their bond, permitting them to ride back through a sleeping camp. No cheering crowd greeted them as it had after Senec's previous marriages and the tent remained undecorated, stark and barren. The only sounds they heard were the waking calls of horses and the barking of dogs. When they had dismounted, Donleth brought them chica and that was their wedding feast. But Ganina called to the headman before he left.

"We will require refurbishing for this tent," she told him,

looking questioningly at Senec. He nodded, knowing what was in her mind because they were his thoughts, as well. He would not take his father's tent, only what was in it. "Bring what is needed from the Warlord's tent while I am away with my husband. If anything is lacking, take it from the tent of the wives. Then you may take the red tent down. It is old and may become tattered by the winds."

Donleth stared at her for a moment. "You go to the pasturelands, My Lord?" It was an oblique way of asking if a woman would really accompany men on such a trip…and if he was giving a new wife so much authority, ordering his father's tent dismantled.

But Ganina was not new to that camp. She knew what to do. "Yes," Senec affirmed. "Keep these ponies for us and have others readied for our guests."

Donleth bowed, silently, and departed for a busy morning.

Senec turned to his wife. "Dress for riding," he told her. "It is not a hard ride, but neither is it short, and you will need clothes accordingly. Do you have any?" He knew his father had never let the girl go anywhere.

"I do." Senec hoped she had broken in boots, but somehow he suspected she had. For a long time after her marriage to his father, he had thought she entertained thoughts of escaping back to the north. Now she should be more content. Sex was a powerful hold over a girl as young and newly-awakened as Ganina. He could hold her with that, at least for a while.

Chapter Seven

Ifelsten opened his eyes on a groan. The vast expense of tent above him was unfamiliar and he cocked his head experimentally, trying to gauge the distance to the apex. That was when he realized exactly how drunk he had been. His head felt like the inside of a drum, but he would be expected to get up that morning and ride one of those furry-assed little Covetian ponies. Abruptly, he retched.

When he had rid himself of what seemed like half a flask of putrid Covetian wine, he lay back, panting. What in the name of the unholy did they put in that stuff? He had tasted no rotgut like that since his early days in the port cities of Westenia. Of course, he had been young then and thought he was immortal, pouring the stuff down like it was water and waking up in alleys. But now, improbably, he looked likely to be Chief of Westenia. The only other logical candidate for the title was busy planting something. After mapping out a military campaign, manufacturing lightning fire, leading troops and spilling an alarming quantity of his Juragian blood on Westenian soil, his friend Caln who had fought alongside him had calmly gone back to farming and fathering more children. Ifelsten shook his head, winced and cursed.

He had wanted Caln to come with him to deal with Caln's half-brother, Senec, but there was a new baby and the corn had to be planted. By the gods, Caln had given him every excuse known to man and a few more. Finally, even Ifelsten had to give up. When Caln would not be moved, he would not. But that had stood them in good stead during the uprising against Covetia, so Ifelsten supposed he could not begrudge the man a bit of peace afterwards.

For himself, Ifelsten knew, there would be none. They had held Senec prisoner for a time after he had led twenty-three Warlords' sons and a horsemaster into their country, thinking it would be easy to subdue. Ifelsten had taken his measure then. Senec was a capable leader. It was his over-confident father who had sent him into unexpected lightning fire used by men so desperate for freedom that they threw themselves onto spears, trying to reach the enemy. Instead of covering themselves with glory, Senec's men had died and he had lived only by the grace of his dead horse falling on him. Ifelsten's men had thought he was dead, too, when they pulled him out. Then someone noticed he did not look Covetian. Someone else heard him ask for Caln. Providentially, no one had killed him and now, after nearly two years in which his father and brother had constantly undermined the peace treaty, Senec was the leader of his land's most influential clan. He was a force to be reckoned with, and it was up to Ifelsten to do the reckoning. Unfortunately, all Westenia's chief wanted to do at that moment was to puke again.

Finally, he pulled himself together and staggered to the tent flap. Why could these people not have doors like anyone else? He had used his pisspot for other purposes and there were no trees. Intent upon relieving himself, he had to wend a painful way to the horses and pee amongst them. He patted his chestnut gelding by way of apology. The horse was too worn to use that day. But they had ridden hard to Covetia upon receiving Senec's invitation. It did not do to keep bodies waiting too long, even if the tribesmen had used an ice house for storage.

That must have been a feat, Ifelsten admitted— transporting those bodies and keeping them in condition for sky burial. Then again, who knew what condition they were in beneath all the fine trappings? Small wonder those priests had used so much incense and thank fate the wind had been blowing the other way, strongly...well, except for that one puff up the face, as if the spirit of Atulfa defied them even in death. From all he had heard of the old man, Ifelsten thought it likely.

Hopefully, Senec would be easier to deal with. At the moment, with fully half his population dead of battle or starvation, he had no choice. But the Covetians still had their tough little women, already breeding. In another fifteen years, they would have produced a new army, and Senec was still young.

Senec wanted coal. Ifelsten was no envoy like the Juragian, but he knew damn well Senec wanted coal and why. The Covetians had horses half the world coveted and with iron shoes from coal-fired forges, those horses could overrun it. With iron and carbon shaped over those same forges, Senec could have steel for swords and other weapons. They would have to fight Covetia again someday.

Meanwhile, Ifelsten thought, if he could plant an army of Westenian settlers along the border, they would be shock troops. It would be move/countermove, match and point, thrust and parry for years. He needed Caln or someone equally capable along that border to keep an eye on things. But he feared Caln would remain immovable, married to his land and the despoiled priestess he had wed. The man was so bloody unworldly he had given fifteen years' accumulated gold coin from his winter trapping to Senec, saying his half-brother needed the money more than he did. Well, Ifelsten intended to return to Westenia with his purse a great deal heavier. Loans should be repaid.

The Covetians would get coal, one way or another. He could give it to them and get valuable grazing land and an alliance, or let them get it from the Juragians and have to fight them that much sooner. It was why Lembach was there, of course. Juragia had stayed out of the Westenian uprising, content to watch while it sat on its own supply of lightning fire. Only the fact that Caln's Juragian mother had given him the formula for that had saved their Westenian hides. It was his good fortune, Ifelsten knew, that Atulfa's hostility after Caln's mother died had driven the younger man straight into their arms. Caln had joined the

Covetians settling their newly-conquered territory, Westenia. When his settler neighbors decided to murder him and take his land, though, they had tangled with the wrong man. Caln had thrown in his lot with Ifelstein and co-led the revolt.

Juragia had taken no part, but now their envoy was in place, ready to make the most of the outcome. Ifelsten had no idea what Senec proposed to barter with Lembach...perhaps passage through one or two of the northern passes, unlocking Juragia's southern border. He didn't care where the damn Juragians did or did not go or by whose leave. He didn't like them. But in a sneaky, reluctant sort of way, he did like Senec, who had shown himself to be a man of his word during his enforced stay in Westenia. If you could trust a man who was your prisoner but walked around free, bound by his promise not to try to escape...well, those were good odds.

The Covetians had distant territories in a state of rebellion now that the Warlords had had their teeth pulled and it was for those lands that Senec needed iron-shod horses and swords of steel. That they might later be turned against Westenia was a thing he must consider, of course. But if he could populate the border and garrison it strongly enough, he might in turn pull Senec's teeth—at least for a while. No peace was ever permanent. No one expected it to be.

There was a stirring then from some of the smaller tents where men traveling with him had slept, most of them with

Covetian women. Ifelsten could see their small forms scurrying off into the morning and shook his aching head. They repulsed him. Had someone offered the copper-haired girl, he would have taken her; she did not resemble the brown-skinned southern Covetian females. But he thought that one had spent her night with Senec. Too bad.

Valdorn, second in command since Caln had embraced the rustic life, stumbled out and over to him. Bleary-eyed and unshaven, he was in no better condition than his leader.

"Hard night, eh?" Ifelsten smirked, and the younger man chuckled.

"They fuck like rabbits."

"No doubt," Ifelsten mused, not especially concerned about his lieutenant's nocturnal activities.

"None for you, I see."

"I can't get past the look of them." Ifelsten shrugged. "The red-haired girl was all right, but not the others."

"Well, she won't be back." Valdorn was good at acquiring intelligence; that was why Ifelsten had picked him to watch his back. "My translator says Senec married her this morning when the sun was hardly up. Must've been a good night."

"Do they really do that?" Ifelsten asked in distaste. "Marry their father's wives?"

"Apparently." Valdorn had obviously pursued a relationship with his translator. It was hard to find men on the border who spoke both tongues, since the populations disliked each other so much. When you did, though, they were valuable sources of information. "He won't take the older ones, but he's stuck with them. He just took pick of the litter."

"I should say so." Ifelsten had liked the look of that girl, and her spirit. She had borne hunger, discomfort and abuse without a word, though she had looked done in at the funeral. Still, she had come around quickly enough when he kicked her. And there had been a spark of attraction...and gratitude. Even without speaking her language, he had felt that clearly. They would have made a good night of it, too.

But status wouldn't save his balls if he tried to have a Warlord's wife.

"Better look over those ponies," he advised Valdorn. "That's what we'll be riding today, unfortunately."

"Think you can get pasture lands?"

Ifelsten nodded. "Keep a sharp eye out for good territory as we pass over it. It has to be contiguous with our border. If Senec is as smart as I think he is, he'll treat with me and Lembach both, but so long as we get land we can settle, I don't care. The Juragians pose no threat to us unless they can get all the way through Covetia, and even weakened as it is, I doubt they can. They say the northern Covetian warlords were untouched by this thing and there are thousands of tribesmen up there, all of them just itching to kill something. Lightning fire or no, Lembach's people will have to tread carefully. Those warlords know they have it. They won't be taken by surprise like the ones who invaded Westenia."

"No, and they can do plenty of damage with those crossbows of theirs in the mountain passes," Valdorn agreed. "Covetia is still dangerous."

"I want a settlement treaty on top of the peace treaty," Ifelsten told him. "Senec should be willing to leave us alone for a while. He needs to go to his territories to keep tribute money coming. Right now, they think they can defy him. Let him get some of his northern brethren and give them swords forged over Westenian coal and that will change in a hurry. That's really why he married the girl. They say her father commands thousands of men along the border."

"Yep." Valdorn yawned, but he had already turned to look over the nearby pony herd. "Senec will make a treaty with the Juragians to keep them off his back and then take our coal, make weapons in a hurry and fall on those other poor bastards just the way his father would have."

Ifelsten shivered slightly despite himself. The original invasion of Covetia had taught him what those methods entailed. Without Caln and his lightning fire, Westenia would still be a territory of Atulfa's people.

"I don't doubt that Lembach has brought a bit of bribe money with him, knowing he's up against us." He smiled coolly at his lieutenant. "We'll let him go first. Time to get Caln's loan back."

Chapter Eight

The grasslands waved green and gilt, a living tide of wind-driven grasses whipping softly about the knees of passing ponies. Ganina viewed their splendor in innocent wonder, questioning in her mind why Senec did not make camp here. More rain fell in the lowlands. The grass was succulent and occasionally she could hear a distant chuckle of water from some small stream or rill. They had nothing like it in the dry highlands where the Camp of the Horsetails made its semi-permanent home. The grass there, while sufficient, did not feed their animals as this would have done. And though they had a shallow, brackish water source that passed for a river, the lively sounds of running liquid silver in the lowlands made her long for a bath in their waters. She wondered if she could convince Senec to try one before they left.

He had given her the black pony, which she rode close beside his bay mare. It was a fine, spritely animal and Ganina rode well…or she always had, anyway. Two years afoot had taken her riding legs from her, but more or less free upon a pony and confronted by open land, she quickly remembered that she came from a nomadic people. Her heart rose on such a swell that she thought it might burst. To one side, she felt the Westenian chief studying her as he had the night before, but she paid him no heed.

The man on the other side, who had left her so sore that riding was a bittersweet pleasure, was her husband. Her husband, who had gratified first her body and now her taste for freedom. Passing beneath the great blue dome of Covetian sky, she liked him well enough.

"There." Senec pointed towards the sentinel, a silver-white stallion who had taken the high ground and now bugled a challenge at the ponies. His cry was curiously commingled with lust and longing, however. The Covetians brought pony mares in season when they wished to round up some of their larger mounts and the stallion had grown accustomed to being offered one of them and some coveted food in exchange for approaching humans. Pony boys always accompanied the herds, maintaining ties with some of the gentler mares and handling new foals so that they knew human scent from birth. The horses were only half-wild, like their masters.

Ganina saw that she had lost the attention of the Westenian. His gaze riveted on the horse herd like a man dying of thirst sighting a spring. They were a lovely sight—a patchwork of gray and bay, bright chestnut and the occasional gold, piebald and dun. A sea of graceful legs churned long grasses as they trotted forward en masse for a look at the approaching ponies. Their heads were high, their eyes bright beneath flowing forelocks. Senec's people had bred them time out of mind, for longer than anyone remembered, until they epitomized grace and power harnessed to the will of man. If you could catch them, that was.

But the pony boys whose lives were spent with them always did. Accepted by the horses as a part of the herd, they caught a few of the mares who had been left haltered and the stallion came skidding in among them, grunting and reeking of hot sweat. The mares skittered sideways, intimidated by his show of force, but the boys met him with chunks of bread and a coquettish little bay pony mare who swirled her rump in his face. She had played this game with him many times and had offspring to prove it. Snatching bread from one of the laughing boys, the stallion mounted the much smaller mare, plunging into her so hard two of the boys had to brace her shoulders, ducking to avoid the stallion's forefeet.

Seizing upon his inattention, the other boys ran fearlessly among the milling horses, pulling out selected mares. Most of them had foals or yearlings at the side and all were heavily pregnant again.

"We will take these to an enclosed area until they have foaled," Senec explained through his interpreter. "We also have two and three-year-olds there for breaking, and those we have gelded. They would not survive a challenge from the stallion."

"I can see that," Ifelsten breathed, watching the impressive animal who had finally dismounted from his mare and was trotting in a possessive circle around her, nostrils flaring, long mane rising and falling in time with his motion. Though the boys still had a long tether on the mare, they stood well back. Unconcerned, the little bay dropped her head, starting to graze. Eventually, her lack of reaction would calm the stallion and he would return to his somewhat reduced herd until he wanted her again.

Ganina felt the palms of her hands grow sweaty, watching the still half-erect horse whose heavy testicles swung against his flanks as he trotted, and the little mare standing unconcerned as semen dripped from her puckered vulva. She caught the tension in Senec's profile; he was obviously thinking exactly what she was. Beneath their loose cotton trousers, Ganina knew, every man watching that mare being bred was at least half-hard; every one of them looked at her, covertly. But to her face, now they could show only respect. She would never again be called a slut, not by anyone. To insult the wife of the tribal leader was to invite death at his hand and she had not the slightest doubt Senec would uphold her honor, just as he would kill her if she betrayed his. So she took care not to look at the Westenian chief who had shown her kindness. She did glance at the Juragian, but his expression remained the same as always, as if he had smelled something slightly off.

"Come," Senec extended an invitation to Ifelsten through the interpreter. Ganina noticed Lembach did not appear to be included. "Let us follow the boys. There is a three-year-old I wish you to see. Though he is but newly broken, I think he might suit you."

Ifelsten's astonishment showed. Though a Covetian in a good mood might offer you a pony, to be given a member of their prized horse herd was high honor indeed. To the accompaniment of the merry jingle of bells left on them to quickly identify foaling mares, the line of visitors set out at a sedate walk to paddocks where those mares would be put to await safe delivery of their precious cargo. They carried a large portion of the wealth of the tribe, had Senec ever cared to sell them. But even in the time of greatest extremity, not one had been sold. Now he gave one to Westenia.

"You can ride him back to your country," Senec said, dismissing Ifelsten in a single sentence. He turned to Lembach, who was waiting at vulture-like attention.

"But you, I think, are not a horseman," he said through the interpreter, and Ganina bit back laughter. It was a deadly insult, but the Juragian only smiled, gratified to have his host's attention. "We will have other areas of interest in common."

"Indeed," Lembach agreed. "I daresay Lord Ifelsten has better use for a good mount."

"Just as you say." Senec nodded complacently. "You must bide with us for a day or two before you undertake your long journey. Our Westenian neighbors, however, will depart in the morn if I am not mistaken."

"At first light," Ifelsten agreed, rather shortly, and Ganina did not miss the fleeting expression of triumph on Lembach's face. It appeared her husband was giving the nod to Juragia, with a generous gift to Westenia to soften the blow. She was surprised, but no doubt he had his reasons. It was not her place to comment. The one thing she did understand was that somehow, without ever seeming to do it, Senec had maneuvered his beggared country into the position of giving or withholding. It was astounding. Atulfa could not have done it in his best days.

But the rule of Atulfa was indeed ended and Ganina had the notion that the rag-tag camp she had despised was going to change. People who had eaten rats and grass would rise again to a position of power under Senec. She clucked her willing pony to a position at his heel.

Chapter Nine

Ifelsten's head had finally stopped pounding by the time they returned to the main camp. A fine young son of the silver stallion followed his little chestnut pony on a tether, curveting and snapping at his mount, and it claimed his attention. Gods, it would be a relief to ride something that didn't make him feel like his feet were dragging on the ground. Of course, it might be his ass on the ground; his new horse hadn't been broken for long and Senec grinned at him, a white flash of teeth through beard. The translator pulled back a moment, apparently conveying a message from the Warlord, and Ifelsten forced himself to assume an unpained expression. Secretly, he feared the young stallion might pull his arm from its socket.

"Lord Senec bids you join him in the red tent upon returning," the obsequious man half-lisped. He had done an adequate job, yet Ifelsten found he could not like the translator. There was something unwholesome about him. Still, the message was of great interest. If he was not mistaken, this invitation did not include the Juragian party. What was Senec up to?

Lembach seemed complacent, since he understood no Westenian. If he had comprehended that message, Ifelsten thought, the Juragian would have been shitting turds. But it probably appeared to him that the translator was making some joke about the horse.

It was a long ride under a hot sun with the fractious animal in tow. Ifelsten was not sorry to have Aben the pony boy run directly to him when they reached camp, eyes wide with admiration for the horse he led. The boy was a hard little worker, Ifelsten thought, and slipped him a copper penny—great riches in Covetia.

"Ask him to see to the care of this horse and have it ready to travel at dawn," he instructed the translator. The boy nodded enthusiastic compliance. When Ifelsten slid from the chestnut pony, which wasn't much of a drop, Aben was quick to take the reins of that one, too.

Ifelsten did not ask any of his men to accompany him, though he noticed the translator fall into step behind him as he strolled with studied casualness towards the red tent. Once the scene of most camp activities, it stood like an old, dying animal silhouetted against the bright sky and sere grass. Entering, Ifelsten was stunned. The thin ochre walls rippled with air currents, but inside there was not one thing. It was stripped bare and he knew at once his sense of its demise was justified. Senec was going to tear down his father's tent, which had symbolized the might of Atulfa. It was a powerful signal of who was now in charge.

Senec was there, pacing the circumference of the tent as if measuring it or, perhaps, bidding it farewell. Ifelsten knew that of fifty warriors Senec had led into Westenia, he had chosen to give sky burial to only one—the horsemaster who had served his family for virtually an entire lifetime. Senec had faithfully tended that man's bier, carefully dismantling the bones when they were sun-cured, placing them in a red silk sack stowed behind the cantle of his saddle. The bag had probably been meant for Senec's bones, Ifelsten thought, if it came to that. But he had reverently taken those of his family's faithful servant—the one man without choice—and carried them to Covetia for consecration in the Ancestor Cave. He knew Senec was not in his father's tent without a reason.

The Warlord's brooding look dissipated quickly, however, at the entrance of his guest and the translator.

"Ah, Lord Ifelsten," he said quietly. "Quite a change since yesterday, is it not?" He gestured at the cavernous tent while the interpreter conveyed his thoughts.

"Indeed. Will you let your father's tent now rest?"

"That is a gracious way to express it. Yes, I will ask the women to dismantle this by sundown."

Ifelsten briefly touched one time-worn wall. "A thing of importance should end with dignity. This tent will not long survive Atulfa, by the look of it."

"I think he planned it that way." Senec nodded. "Often we urged him to have a new one raised, but he would not do it. I see now what was in his mind." He sighed, and Ifelsten wondered if he regretted his father's death…if he had caused it. It was not a thing he could ask through the translator, though if they had been able to speak directly, he might have dared. This was Caln's brother, after all, and the two of them had shared food at the same hearth.

"What is in *your* mind?" he finally settled for asking.

"Your travel tomorrow." Senec replied promptly. "You should make good time on that horse. And back again."

"Back again?"

"I will meet now with Lembach. Our business will not take long. He will dicker for right of passage through our northern passes. Which I will give him. It is what he wants, so he will go quickly." He smiled his infrequent, oddly charming smile. "I will have money for my brother in the morning. Take it to him for me. When you have rested for a time, return here. We will speak of the land you want. I need coal, Ifelsten. Give me that and access to your port, and land along my border is yours."

"My price is thirty thousand acres, contiguous with Westenia's border."

Senec raised one eyebrow. "That is a round number. For how much coal?"

"Sufficient for your needs for three years," Ifelsten replied. "You have people to warm and forges to supply. I may have trouble convincing my counselors to allow you access to our port, though."

Senec spread his hands, expressively. "We are landlocked here. It will be a constant bone of contention if we cannot pass freely."

"For commerce?" Ifelsten's eyes narrowed. "Let us be frank. You need passage for troops to pacify your territories. The sight of armed Covetian troops passing through Westenia will provoke panic."

"We can go overland." Senec didn't even try to deny his intent. "And return by sea. We will have ships then. Half of them will be yours when we dock."

So, he planned to attack the Sowetians first and from the north. Through Juragia. Ifelsten had to stifle a smile. Senec would gather fighters from his wife's father in the north, go through the pass so newly shared with Juragia and down the finger of land into Sowetia. It was sparsely populated, so not many Juragians would complain. Sowetia would not expect the northern assault and Senec would firestorm his way through to the southern port, seizing their ships as tribute and sailing his men and horses home via Westenia, which had no treaty with Sowetia. Leaving behind a fleet of the finest ships in any of the territories, half of them signed over to Ifelsten's people.

"I think I can quell the panic," Ifelsten said. He felt the certainty in his gut that had never yet misled him, taking him from wastrel to chieftain in only a few short years. He must trust it...must trust Senec. Still, the other man was young. He might make mistakes. "Make no agreement with Lembach that denies you the right to treat with us."

Senec glanced at him sharply. "I will treat with whomever I wish," he responded. "Always."

Ifelsten knew he did not imagine the note of warning in Senec's voice. Not so young or foolish, then.

"Good," he said. "I will see your brother and return before the new moon. Lembach should be halfway to the passes by then."

"Perhaps not quite so far," Senec differed. "We will have to be careful not to trample him on our way."

Ifelsten laughed. Covetians on horseback covered land at a pace no one could believe until they saw it.

The conversation had reached a momentary lull, but then Senec turned his attention to the translator they had kept so busy.

"Mermet, my thanks," he said, reaching for the other man's hand. "You have given good service."

The little man smiled tightly, but let himself be taken in his Warlord's congratulatory grip—a grip like iron. His eyes widened, apprehending danger too late as—fast as a snake striking—Senec whipped a dagger from his waistband and slit the smaller man's throat in a motion Ifelsten's gaze could barely follow. The translator's knees buckled as blood sprayed onto the soil of the tent floor, which sucked it up hungrily. Ifelsten felt a rush of battle strength, leaping clear of the fountain of blood. Clear of Senec's reach, as well.

"What in the name of the gods…" he began, but then stopped. They had no translator now.

Senec bent to push his knife into the earth, cleaning it, leaving himself unarmed and his back as a target. Ifelsten could see Caln's brother breathing heavily, clearly aware of his own danger. When no attack came, Senec straightened up and sheathed his blade in its hiding place. He looked at the body, then at Ifelsten, and shrugged.

"Go Lembach," he said in the bit of fractured Westenian Caln had been able to teach him. "For money."

Yes, Ifelsten thought. The little worm at their feet would have gone straight to Lembach with the information he had just translated and been handsomely rewarded.

"Come back," Senec went on, casually kicking dirt over the worst of the mess. "Soon."

Chapter Ten

Summer had come to the Camp of the Horsetails. Senec had refused to remove to the cooler lowlands, saying lush grass there would founder his tough ponies, accustomed to hard foraging. Sickened by rich green grass, they would become lame and useless, so the tribe would go in the fall when the grass had faded, driving carts with new iron-rimmed wheels thanks to the receipt of Westenian coal. That was why Ganina sat on a seat of fur beside her tent watching heat shimmer over the tawny plain, sparking an occasional dust devil. Wild hawks sailed on thermals, cruising in lazy expectation of a meal. Animals driven to the comfort of the river provided easy plunder. As long as it did not go dry, those hawks would live well, as would the ones hunting for the tribe.

Thus far, the river had been generous. It had been a bountiful season—not as good as before war with Westenia, but welcome. Boys who had been young when their country was crushed were growing into hunters, while smaller boys and girls now were old enough to serve as beaters for the circle hunts used when there were not enough men. They hunted everything on the plains for many miles around and there were fewer people to feed, with the warriors gone.

Ganina was flourishing, too, suffering only from the absence of her husband—gone to meet with her father and thence to war. Though he had erected her own tent behind his, she spent most nights with him. Now, she missed him in her bed. Not yet with child, she was anxious to conceive one, though Senec appeared unconcerned. Of course, he had Gilya. She smiled at the little boy, playing with cornstalk horses in the dust. At last the memory of his mother seemed to be fading and the child was more content, accepting Ganina in her place.

He loved those horses. Ifelsten had brought them on his return trip—an uncommonly thoughtful gesture for a man with no family. Ganina reflected upon that for a moment, with pensive longing she recognized as mere curiosity about what might have been. Most likely, she thought with a sigh, she would have been foreign and unwelcome in his country and found she shared nothing with him. At least with Senec she remained among Covetians bound to show her respect, as her husband did. He had been good to her, giving her whatever she wanted except any inkling of how his mind worked or what he felt.

Instead she had spacious shelter, a fine pony, clothes and beads and jewels, serving women and a nursemaid for the child. Her life was easy—a veritable paradise compared to existence as Atulfa's wife. Senec showed her honor in public and had left her with responsibilities and authority in his absence. She thought perhaps if she had a child upon which to shower the love he didn't want, she might be happy.

In the meantime, little Gilya needed her. He was a moody child, much like his father in that way, but of course he had lost his mother. Thinking it, Ganina went to collect him.

"What have you named your horse?" she asked, stroking his hair.

"Jenko," he responded instantly, looking up at her with typical round, brown southern Covetian eyes just like his mother's. She smiled. It was the name of the gray horse Senec had given to Ifelsten. Like her, the child had been taken with the blond chieftain who was now an ally. So well did the Westenian and Covetian leaders get along that Senec's returning troops were expected to pass through the lower part of Westenia. It was expected that Senec would maintain iron control over his men, and Ifelstein could not help it if local commanders had armed troops posted every step of the way. He had given them that authority, after all. Senec—served by a new translator since his appeared to have vanished—had agreed to everything.

Now, all there was to do was wait. With Donleth to organize the men and boys and Ganina's strong hand over the women, the camp and herds had never looked better.

"Would you like to go hawking tomorrow?" Ganina asked the little boy, and his head bobbed immediately. Like all small boys, Gilya had a pony, which he could ride on a tether, and his own little merlin, though Donleth would carry it. The merlin would bring down minor game birds that would be Gilya's first kills for the tribe. Ganina knew his father would be pleased.

"All right," she said. "Donleth and one of the boys will come. Perhaps we could ask Aben. It will give him a rest from the ponies."

"Yes!" Gilya agreed enthusiastically. He often spent time with Aben, currying ponies and picking burrs out of their manes and tails.

"In the meantime…" Ganina teased, taking his small hand in one of hers and the fox fur she had sat on in the other. "We will have a nap. It's very hot. When we get up it will be cooler and I will give you cold tea."

"Now?" the child questioned with a sly grin. She felt a pang; that grin reminded her of Senec. Gilya looked more Covetian than his father because he was. Still, there were strong, frequent flashes of his paternity in the child. "I'm hot NOW!"

Ganina laughed, pleased that he was making any demands upon her. For a long time, he had barely spoken. "So am I. Come to my tent and we will have some."

They did, using precious ice from the northern ice houses, and the long, lazy afternoon commenced. Drowsing with the child on her comfortable bed, she was suffused with a sense of well-being. She knew every sound in the camp: the bleats and calls of goats, snorts of ponies, the occasional yip of a dog, an occasional murmur of voices. They soothed her as she drifted into sleep. Not everyone could afford the luxury of a nap during the heat of the day. But she was the Warlord's wife.

Wrongness of sound awakened her. The bleats of goats were like the panicked cries of lost souls and dogs were snarling and yelping. Abruptly, her tent flap opened. Ganina stared up at Donleth, wide-eyed, not yet willing to speak because the child still slept.

"Horses," the headman said tersely. "Not ours."

"What—?" she stuttered, numb with sleep.

"It's a raid."

"A raid?" Ganina knew she was repeating herself, but it was nearly beyond comprehension. The Northern warlords had gone with Senec. Those to the middle and south of their country had remained, all of them signatories to an alliance with the Camp of the Horsetails and Westenia. Weren't they?

"Who—?" she stumbled again, but Donleth was pulling Senec's son from her grasp, stilling his sleepy protest with a hand over his mouth.

"Silence!" he commanded the child in the way all Covetian children were taught.

"Not all have signed," he went on. "Illinea's and Drusa's fathers have not." In the distance, Ganina could hear pounding hooves and shouts, and Donleth nodded shortly at the little boy in his arms. "Drusa's father has come for his grandson."

"They will kill me," Ganina comprehended at once. Her

blood was turned to ice as she recalled Illinea's threats.

"Yes." Donleth tore down a bundle she had scarcely noticed, strapped to a centerpost. Tossing it to her, he bundled Gilya in a soft wool wrap, effectively binding him. The child, well-schooled by his father, had not uttered a word. "We do not have men enough to hold them off. You must take Gilya and two ponies and ride for the Westenian border. Gallop the first one till it drops, then take the second. We will delay them as long as possible. Westenian troops kill anyone trying to cross the border, but they know you are Senec's wife. Have them take you to Ifelsten. Our troops will be returning through Westenia and will avenge us."

"Gods, Donleth," Ganina uttered hopelessly. But the old warrior did not want her pity. His teeth flashed briefly against his weathered skin in a fierce grin.

"It will be good to kill again." He pushed her through the tent flap. "Now GO!"

Like a frightened animal, she scuttled behind the ridge concealing the pony herd, clutching Sennec's son to her. Every man, woman and child in the camp had turned out, armed with anything they could get their hands on, but they would all die that afternoon. Aben knew it, but ran as fast as his bony bare feet would carry him towards her with the black pony and another in tow. There had not been time to saddle them, but no Covetian ever needed a saddle. Handing Gilya to the not-much-bigger pony boy,

Ganina grasped a section of the second pony's mane and swung onto him. Grunting with effort, Aben hoisted Gilya behind her and strapped the child to her body with desperate haste, using the throw in which Donleth had wrapped him.

"Your pack!" the boy gasped, and Ganina snatched the bundle Sennec's headman had provided, wondering what it contained...why it had been secreted in her tent. Had Donleth, wise in the ways of treachery, suspected enemies would strike in her husband's absence? Had Senec—too confident, too arrogant as his father sometimes had been—killed her and the others by leaving an insufficient guard?

Whoops and screams pre-empted other thoughts. "Go, lady!" the boy urged, and Ganina booted the bay pony, feeling her arm jerk with the yank of the black gelding's tether stretching taut. Then both ponies were streaking for the outskirts of the camp, straight for the lowlands and Westenia.

She rode like the hand of death pursued her, while behind her Aben and another boy drove the herd, screaming and pelting them with rocks so that they galloped between her and enemies streaming into the camp. It was too much to hope they had not seen her, but the living tide of ponies was impenetrable and there was no immediate pursuit. Lighter and faster than any man, Ganina rode for her life with every bit of skill and cunning bred into the daughter of a mountain warlord. The black pony followed almost without need for a tether, so close that his hooves cut the shadow of the other animal. Although Ganina could feel Gilya's small arms pressed against her ribs, gripping the cloth of her blouse, Donleth's instruction held him silent. The child's cooperation would not last indefinitely, but for the moments she needed, it sufficed.

"AYAHH!" she screamed into the bay pony's ear, kicking furiously. Though she wore only kidskin slippers donned for sleep, he stretched into headlong flight so fast that she felt the chafe of windburn across her face. He could not maintain it for long, but she needed only a head start. After that, she needed to find a short cut to the lowlands over rocky and difficult places where she might outdistance the other riders handicapped by unfamiliarity with the terrain. Though she felt Gilya's slight form pressed against her, she had no time for him. There was no time for anything but smelling the reek of sweat from her galloping pony, hearing the startled whoosh of birds spooked by his passage, the rush of wind and the thunder of her terrified heart.

Chapter Eleven

Pursuit was a small, indistinct line along the horizon—too far away to make out individuals. But it wasn't riders to the rear Ganina feared. Gilya's presence strapped to her back insured no one would shoot her. Instead, she knew, they would try to outflank her ponies and shoot them. Her only hope was to stay so far ahead that they couldn't, and her only strength was that of the animal beneath her. He was still fleeing so fast she could discern no stride, but ponies were bred for endurance, not speed. When she saw that the riders were not gaining on her, she ceased urging him, letting him settle to a fast but not frantic pace. Already she could see cream-colored foam dripping from both animals and her seat was growing more precarious against the sweat-slick coat of the bay pony. It took every bit of her balance and concentration to stay with him, but if she fell, she was already dead. Just like at Atulfa's funeral, to falter was to perish. She wondered whether Ifelsten could save her again.

She cut a path cut straight across the plain, using the sun and her memory for guides. After a short time, however, she began to suspect the ponies remembered their trip to the lowlands, too. With very little guidance, the bay gelding charted a course to the place where he had found good grass and the company of a horse herd. His cooperation enabled her to fumble one-handed in the pack she had belted to her skirt. She prayed Donleth had included water.

He had. Inside were water, dried meat and boots. That was all, but it was enough. Uncorking the waterskin, she drank sparingly, cautious about spilling a single drop, but the vessels of her people were well designed for use while riding. Warriors often had to eat, drink and even perform bodily functions on horseback. Of course, men had some advantage there. She was not sure what she would do if she had to pee, but she was too frightened just then to feel the need. She dared not stop to give water to Gilya and the inability ate her heart to the core.

After a while the pony was less willing, but time had ceased to have meaning for Ganina. She had no idea how long she had run him because it didn't matter. He would have to die and then she had to hope the black pony, the stronger animal of the two, would have enough left in reserve to get her to the border.

Her focus narrowed to a bizarre reverie, deceptively calm. Barely-familiar scenery passed in a nearly flat line, summer-sere grass gradually giving way to greener foliage and occasional bushes she avoided like grim death. Animals would have dug burrow-holes there, in the shade. A single misstep in one of those and her mount was doomed.

Instead she urged him with increasing urgency down, down, down the long incline to the lowlands. Even with gravity in his favor, he was starting to lag. He would have been only too happy of a rest and she thanked the tenacious spirit of the black pony who nipped at his flanks when he slowed. She suspected it was simply a game between them, but one never knew. She liked that black pony and he seemed to like her, and sometimes she did wonder how much the animals knew. Could he smell fear on her? Did he sense what he would be asked to do?

Shadows lengthened. She could no longer see the men behind her so distinctly, but not because they were falling back...it was because sunset would give them concealment. She had to be at the border by then. If she ran that pony in darkness, she would lose her direction and he would surely break a leg. After hours of all-out effort, he was chuffing and wheezing and Gilya—as though sensing the animal's distress—started to cry.

"Silence!" Ganina roared in her best imitation of Senec and Donleth, but the child was not fooled. She wasn't a man and he continued to sob in a choking cacophony that strained her nerves to breaking. He needed water, he needed rest and care and not to expend his energy. "Gilya, don't cry," she pleaded above the laboring breath of the pony. Even the black pony was rolling his eyes, trailing sweat into the now-knee high grass. "We will stop soon."

It mollified him for a few moments, but of course she didn't stop. Instead, she began to lash the bay as his stride shortened and blood-tinged foam blew into her face. The membranes of his lungs were rupturing. The black pony began to pass him and that was when Ganina finally pulled up, searching the horizon behind her in a state of mortal fear. She could not see riders and did not know if she had lost them or they were circling to intercept her. But she could not let the pony fall with her; Gilya would be crushed.

"Hush," she scolded, transferring him in a single motion to the black pony. She had to drop the tether, but the gelding was beyond moving. Even as she got the child off the bay, that one grunted and dropped, flanks heaving, nostrils running bright blood. He would die, but she had no knife to ease his passing. All she could do was take a moment to fall on her knees beside him. His eyes closed and she slicked the soaked forelock off his face long enough to gently circle the white star on his forehead.

"Thank you, my friend," she whispered, and then lurched to her feet with tears running down her own face in defiance of the instruction she had given Gilya. Neither of them could afford to lose water, but she could not stop herself. With a last look at the dying pony, she swung atop the other one, pausing only to pull the waterskin from her pack and give a drink to the child. He drank as children do—clumsily and thirstily, seemingly without end. Ganina restrained a scream of impatience, and at last jerked the skin away.

"I am sorry," she said, secreting the nearly-empty vessel and picking up the black pony's reins. "We will drink again at the border."

Gilya snuffled; the word border had no meaning for him and his time spent with Aben had taught him they were leaving a sick pony—a heinous crime.

"No, no!" he screamed in protest, but Ganina set her heels to the flanks of her favorite pony and prayed.

"We must go, Gilya," she insisted, knotting the throw tightly around her to prevent him leaping. "That pony can rest now. It's all right."

The greater strength of an adult prevailed and he lapsed into sullen silence as the black gelding found a last burst of speed to leave his dying friend.

"Go!" Ganina urged, leaning forward to free the pony's driving hindquarters. "You are the best one. Ayah, go, go!"

He proved it within half a mile, sliding rump-first down a nearly vertical slide of rock to the bottom of a ravine. A narrow thread of water silvered through a gorge there; they were nearing the border. It was territory traversed more by Ifelsten's people than anyone else and Ganina hoped fervently that her pursuers did not know how close to rescue she was. Across the borderlands, Westenians had erected a line of wattle-and-daub guardposts—crude but effective. Help was at hand, if only she could reach it.

Behind her she detected the commotion of a party of men and ponies sliding down that steep slope. They could not encircle her, but they were too close and, and, for the first time, she whipped her mount. He was the pride of the herd; it was why Senec had given him to her. Responding with a final burst of speed, he rocketed up onto the flatlands leading to Westenia. The first points of stars were coming out and birds were hushing, only to be jerked out of their twilight peace by the advent of riders at a dead gallop.

"Ayah!" Ganina screamed again and felt the black pony dig into the earth and then leap forward like a trapped deer. That impetus carried him through grasses which parted like the waves of the sea Ganina had never seen. All she wanted to see then was the outline of guard posts manned by soldiers instructed to kill anyone attempting to cross the border. She hoped they might spare a woman bearing a child, although there was no guarantee.

Ahead of her, she saw the first ugly taupe-gray building. It was a mere blot on the landscape, but inordinately precious in her eyes. The thunder of hooves had drawn men—fair-haired Westenian men, well armed and aroused. She couldn't speak their language, but apparently none was needed. A hail of arrows passed over her, bound for the men rapidly gaining on her. She could not help ducking at the noise. Head down, she skidded her pony into the grassy courtyard of the guard post, making no protest when a tall Westenian grabbed at the rein. The pony stopped so fast that his back legs collapsed under him and Ganina and her precious cargo were flung precipitately into the arms of more men as her mount sat on the ground, panting like a dog.

"What is this?" one man demanded in accented Covetian. She took him to be a border-dweller, somewhat familiar with her tongue. He had probably never seen a Covetian from the north and she was grateful he did use her language.

"I am the wife of Senec," she gasped, half-sobbing. "This is his son." Another man was loosing the child from his bindings. "Enemies have destroyed our camp. They seek my life."

"Not anymore," the first man said. Ganina turned to look back. Half a dozen ponies were trotting loose. One rider was still in his saddle, stuck full of arrows, while the rest lay in unmoving humps in the grass. As Ganina watched, the single remaining rider toppled slowly to join his fellows.

"Senec's wife, you say?" The young Westenian peered at her suspiciously. His eyes were very blue, rimmed with red as though irritated by Covetian heat.

"I am his wife!" she repeated adamantly. "I have sat in council with your chief, Ifelsten. Our troops will be crossing the border from Sowetia into your land. I must reach my husband to tell him what has happened! Please, you must help me!"

"All right, all right." Clearly, the foreigner did not want to deal with a woman in hysterics and strode quickly over to an even taller man, gesticulating and rattling off a stream in his own language. Immediately, a recognizable scouting party took shape, flooding across the plain beyond the fallen bodies. They would be looking for signs of additional pursuit. Ganina could only hope killing and looting and raping had amused the others sufficiently to prevent them joining the hunting party.

"Nina?" Coming out of his trance of weariness and thirst, Gilya tugged firmly on her skirt, claiming her attention. "More water! You promised!"

The heat was no longer so brutal, but Ganina felt dry as a bone. She could only imagine what suffering Senec's child was enduring. From the corner of her eye, she saw two soldiers getting her pony up. It was a good sign if he could stand; perhaps he would live. She must make sure she and Gilya did the same.

"Please!" she called to the man who spoke her tongue. "May I have water for the child?"

"Oh…yes…of course." He shouted to another man, who came from the post's well with a dipper in hand. "Are you hurt?" He gestured to the blood flecked over her face and clothes.

"It is from the first pony I rode," she said, kneeling to ladle water into Gilya's mouth, cupping his little chin in one hand to still his eagerness that would waste it. "I killed him."

The Westenians on the border were good horsemen, dependent on their animals for their lives and transport. "I suppose you had to," the young man said, not unkindly.

"More!" Gilya demanded, petulant now that he had her attention. That needed no translation; the Westenian took the dipper with a smile, handing it to the man who had brought it so he could return with a refill. Ganina was still kneeling in front of

Senec's son and gave him water the moment it came.

"Please!" she pleaded again, attending to the little boy but glancing sidelong at the man who was now a translator, whether or not he had started out that way. "Ifelsten has offered us his help in the past. I must go to him!"

The older man who had ordered the scouting party came up to her then, carrying a bucket of water, offering it. She drank with such desperation that she was shaking by the time she finished, and that man spoke at some length to the other one.

"My commander thinks you should rest overnight, at least," the younger soldier translated. "He says your husband hasn't reached our border yet. We would have heard. It won't hurt if you have rest and food and some clean clothing for yourself and the boy. Then we will take you to Shembel."

"All right," she agreed at once. Shembel. That was where Ifelsten was, at the ruins of a great temple the Westenians had chosen as their capitol place. Was it where Senec planned to go? She wasn't sure. But certainly the Westenians had messengers to reach him. She got painfully to her feet, tugging at Gilya's hand, and the two of them followed the young soldier to one of the unprepossessing huts.

Unexpectedly, Ganina found women inside. They were the wives of higher-ranking men, some with children, and welcomed her without reservation, clucking in sympathy and immediately handing Gilya small candies. He and the other children looked at each other curiously. She supposed the fair-haired children had never seen one with brown hair and round, brown eyes, but they were not unfriendly. Would that their elders could learn from them, she thought ruefully.

One of the women was obviously part-Covetian, too, a misplaced person who would find acceptance only along the border. She spoke Ganina's tongue like a native.

"Come along, my dear," she coaxed. "You're done in."

For the first time, Ganina had a moment to appreciate her own state. She smelled strongly of sweat, hers and the ponies'. Her face, hair, hands and clothing were covered with blood and froth. She was filthy, exhausted, and close to weeping from the sheer relief of being safe but also the knowledge of what lay behind her: bodies and ghosts. A few of the women might be kept alive for sport, but it was better to have died. Anyone bearing the same blood as Senec—and he had many brothers and sisters in the camp—would be killed, probably in the most gruesome manner possible if they happened to escape massacre during the first sweep.

She said nothing of this to the kindly woman, but saw by her compassionate expression that the commander's wife knew.

"My name is Leanda," the woman offered. "We will heat water for you and get you bread and tea and something better for your little boy to eat."

"He is not mine," Ganina explained, "only his father's.

That is the problem. His mother was returned to her father's camp in disgrace and it has begun a feud."

"Stupidity," the older woman sniffed, helping Ganina behind a screen where she could disrobe and step into a tub the other women were helping to fill. Another kindly older woman was putting Gilya in a smaller, round tub and for once the child seemed grateful for a bath. The other children had been ordered out, and without their silent watchful presence Gilya began to fade. Ganina could see his eyelids drooping. He could never ride to Westenia that night and travel in the dark was unsafe. No matter how desperate his grandfather was to have him back, Ganina did not think he would confront the Westenians. They had lightning fire capable of blowing every Covetian to pieces and had not hesitated to use it in the past; it was how they had won the war. Ifelsten might be willing to let a half-trusted ally cross part of his land by pre-arrangement, but hostile encroachment on Westenia's border was a different matter. Drusa's and Illinea's fathers could not touch her while she sat in the borderlands. She could have a night's rest.

"It is more than stupid," Ganina agreed, stepping into the tub with a sigh of relief and beginning to soap herself. She could not bear wearing the blood of the dead pony. "They must know what my husband will do to them."

She shuddered to think of it. During the three months in his life and his bed, Ganina had not seen the side of Senec she knew was there, but she supposed that others had. What arrogance, what stupidity, what suicidal insanity made the two warlords attack his camp? He was returning with an army, her father among them. Retribution would be swift and terrible and the mid-Covetian warlords could not hope to prevail. They had ensured their doom, all for a matter of pride, as far as she could see. They had no allies, to her knowledge. Senec would blot them from the earth.

"Maybe they thought they could use the little boy as a bargaining chip," Leanda suggested.

It was not too farfetched a thought, holding Senec's only son hostage in exchange for…what? What did those men want? Something more than repayment for an affront, no doubt. Yes, it made sense. They didn't love the child. They wanted Gilya for blackmail, to bleed Senec dry, rebuilding the wealth and power of their tribes until they supplanted his. Only Donleth's quick thinking and her headlong dash for the border had prevented it. But it was doubly sure the raiders would vent their wrath on Senec's people. There could be none alive now other than herself, the child and the men who rode with her husband. The Camp of the Horsetails had finally been destroyed. Senec's shame would be even greater than that of his father, who had only sent a number of noble sons to their deaths in Westenia and failed to retrieve their bones.

Senec might take his revenge, but he was ruined. She and

Gilya were all he had left.

Chapter Twelve

The morning dawned fair and clear, so peaceful that it made the previous day seem like a bad dream. Just before daybreak, Ganina felt Gilya burrow into her bed like a little animal. When she wakened, he was still there and she smiled, sadly. This was the day she had planned to take him hawking. Instead, she was running for her life, away from the shattered remnants of a people she had thought would rise to power. They would never rise again.

But she did, silently, dressing and going outside. There was no sign of the evening's events, just a few Covetian ponies corralled among larger Westenian horses. She thought she saw the black pony among them and was glad. There were some men on patrol…a small campfire…the crowing of a rooster escalating as the sun gained ascendancy. She was sure that morning looked no different than a hundred others to the Westenians assigned to their isolated outpost. It could not be an easy life. Wattle and daub leaked horribly in the rainy season. They were unaccustomed to the heat of Covetia. Most of all, they were isolated from their people and all the joys of fellowship. They were not just soldiers but pioneers, settlers, alone on a vast expanse of lowland— beautiful but foreign.

"You will have easy travel today." Ganina recognized Leanda's voice behind her and turned with a forced smile. "Did you rest well?"

"Yes," she replied truthfully. She had slept like the dead, exhausted past her mind's ability to keep her wakeful with imagined horrors. That would come later.

"You might as well have food before you go. I know the men aren't going to waste any time getting you into Westenia. I heard them talking about it. They say it will be a while until your troops return from Sowetia and that you will be safest at Shembel until they come."

"Probably," Ganina agreed. "I think Ifelsten will give us sanctuary. He and my husband have always seemed to like one another."

"So I heard." Leanda handed her a mug of tea, ushering her gently back inside where boiled eggs simmered on a coal stove.

"Did Gilya wake yet?" Ganina asked, beginning to eat.

"Ach, no! That child could sleep through a torrent."

"Well, he has suffered a lot. His mother was sent away four months ago. And now this."

"Poor little mite," the commander's wife agreed. "But soon he'll see his father."

"I hope so," Ganina murmured. There was the chance Senec could have been killed in Sowetia, but she doubted it. A warlord was more often involved in directing battle than partaking of it, though he was always a masterful fighter. It was how he gained his position. And she had heard that Senec was superlative. If he had challenged Dyak to combat, the issue between them would have been settled in mere moments. Why had he resorted to poison? She did not consider him the sort of man to take a coward's way, but he had never spoken of it.

What he wanted from her was clear enough: sex and plenty of it, children when they came. He stirred her deeply in their bed. But despite her resolution to have learned it, she still knew nothing of his mind. She knew every inch of his body and nothing of his soul. She supposed that would not have troubled some women, but she had always known she was not like other women. Ganina had always wanted more. It was one reason she disliked her father, who considered her merely something to be bartered. She had not seen him in three years and would not care if she never saw him again. Her mother, dead of some mountain fever, was only a distant memory. She had love to give, long stored up inside of her, and no one who wanted it.

Gilya, she thought, was really the only one who had ever loved her. He came to the interior doorway and then straight to her, climbing directly onto her lap and wrapping his little arms around her neck, head against her shoulder. Her eyes filled with tears as she cuddled him with one arm beneath his backside, the other around his back.

"So, you are awake at last," she teased gently. "We have been waiting for you."

"I sleepy," he muttered, twining his hands in her hair. Gods, Senec did the same in his moments of passion, holding her hair as he thrust into her body. Her insides contracted painfully with the memory.

Well, he was her future, whatever it turned out to be. In the meanwhile, she had his son to care for and took the child outside to the privy. After that, it did not take long to feed the ravenous youngster, and by the time he finished there were men at the door, with tall Westenian horses. They had found her boots and Ganina pulled them on beneath long, light pantaloons one of the women had given her. Her thighs had been abraded, pockmarked red by the friction of riding a pony while dressed in a skirt, and she was happy to have something atop her tender skin. The women had dressed it with some soothing concoction, but it was a long way to Shembel.

The young man who could talk to her rode with her. Leanda's commander husband remained behind, but the men he sent with her were pleasant. To her relief, they didn't question her need to keep Gilya with her and strapped the child to her back just as she had done the previous day. This time, though, Ganina was at pains to reassure him they would ride slowly and give him food and drink to pass the time.

"We are going to see Ifelsten," she cozened him.

"Remember? The man who gave you the horses!"

"They lost," the child pouted.

"I know," Ganina improvised hastily. "We are going to get you more. Bigger ones this time, like these big horses we are riding, see?"

It worked. The child let the men tie him on without protest and she was heartily glad. Those horses were much bigger than her Covetian pony. If either of them fell, it was a long way to the ground.

"My black pony," she said to the young soldier. "Did he live?"

"Yes," he reassured her. "His wind is broken and I don't think he'll ever be good for anything but light work." The man smiled at her. He did not seem to dislike her because she was Covetian, or perhaps it was because she didn't look like one to his inexperienced eye. Probably he had never been more than a few miles from his home; most non-nomadic people hadn't. He would think all Covetians looked like Gilya. "But he got the job done."

"He is a very noble pony," she said seriously. "I will give him a good life if I can take him with me."

"Well, maybe on the way back. He wouldn't make it to Covetia now. We'll take good care of him."

"Thank you," she murmured. Ganina could bear the sight of dead animals needed for food; she was glad to see them in that case. But to kill a pony…that was hard.

The ride settled into what would become a familiar pattern. There was no sign of pursuit, nothing stirred on the border, and after a time of winding their way through upper grasslands they came to a road. Not much of a road, really—just a red clay track. But it was easier going for the horses and they made good time. The men were friendly and cheerful, though the sheer size of them unnerved Ganina.

She was used to Covetian men. Ifelsten was the biggest man she had ever seen and some of these men were even taller. Their long golden hair and fair skins looked peculiar to her; their speech was incomprehensible. She was extremely glad they were no longer enemies, beginning to understand how with the aid of lightning fire they had been able to subjugate her people. It had been foolishness on the part of the warlords, she thought, to ever believe it could work the other way around. These men were strong and they were fighters, not seafarers like the Sowetians or backwards tribes like some others Covetia had subdued. She began to appreciate why Senec considered it more advisable to ally with them. Her father had long since reached the same conclusion about the Juragians, though at one time he had raided them. It would be interesting to see how Senec and her father were getting along. Well enough to fight together, apparently.

She had only her thoughts for entertainment. Without another woman to talk to, it was a long and boring ride, broken up by the need to entertain Gilya. Eventually, the men began handing him around and she sank into apathy, no longer anything but a passenger. She was not sure when they entered Westenia proper— unsure of anything anymore. There was only the hope she had of the two men she must find at the end of her long journey.

* * * *

Ganina had assumed they would not stop except for the hours of darkness, but many days into the ride the young man, Trebew, told her they would be coming to a homestead where she could take a little ease for a while. It was the first item of interest in a vast sea of monotony and she looked at him questioningly.

"We are coming to Caln's Valley," he explained. "We must tell him what has happened."

She felt her heart speed up. Even in Covetia, Senec's half-brother was a legend. He was the man who had given lightning fire to the Westenians and brought about the defeat of her country...Caln, the brat brought to Atulfa's hearth when he married Lorini. People had expected better of him, but what he had given them was death. She had never seen him and didn't want to.

His home lay directly alongside the road. Two piebald horses came charging to the snake-rail fence, making their horses jump aside, while a ferocious-looking gray-brown dog roared a challenge from the house. It was a prosperous looking farm house, white stucco and two stories high, with real glass windows. But despite her need for some comforts, Ganina felt no eagerness to go inside.

The woman who met them did not seem welcoming, either. She was young, with three small children, one still a baby. The dog obeyed her summons and command for silence, but she had nothing to say after that. One of the men spoke to her in Westenian and she gestured towards the fields, indicating that was where Caln could be found. Where else would one find a farmer on a fair day? Eventually she seemed to accede to a request by the men to fetch her husband and sent the oldest child, a girl, towards those fields. With a sense of surprise, Ganina noted that girl was at least partly Covetian. How could it be? The other children were not.

But they were entertainment for Gilya. He kicked and fussed immediately and Ganina put him down with help from one of the men, who lifted him and sent him to the young boy. The smaller baby girl was of no interest, but Gilya showed an immediate inclination to play with the male child. Even then, the mother didn't speak. Not a word. Even when Trebew helped Ganina from her horse and took her up to the blonde-haired woman, she said nothing.

"This is Caln's wife, Delfi," he introduced them. "She doesn't speak, so just manage with her however you can. I told her who you are."

"She can't speak at all?" Ganina could not keep the

surprise from her tone.

"Ah...I don't think so. I never heard her, anyway. We'll stay here overnight."

"Wonderful," Ganina muttered sourly, but she tried giving Delfi a smile. It worked about as well as sunshine melting rock, but Delfi made a motion towards the house and Ganina went in. By that time, she knew she could trust Gilya with the men and a break from his company was welcome. He could be a very demanding child and she was tired.

Inside, she realized she had reached shelter just in time. Her monthly course had come—another month without a baby, since her husband had gone to war. When Delfi's husband came in, she realized very quickly that he would be doing the same.

Like his wife, Caln was quiet. Ganina's first thought was that his eyes were like Senec's, but then she realized they were darker—more sherry-colored than hazel. His hair was darker, too, and curled slightly at the ends. He was tall and fine-boned, with light olive skin, a very good-looking man. She had seen lowland Juragians who looked like him; not all of them were fair. Caln was not like Senec except in one regard—he had Senec's flat, killing look. She saw it overtake him as the men spoke. Without a word, he stood and reached above the fireplace for his broadsword, then turned and walked out the door.

Chapter Thirteen

They had Caln's silent presence for only the first few hours of the trip. Senec's brothers and sisters were also half-siblings to Caln and eventually he could not contain his rage and rode as a Covetian did, outdistancing the rest of the party. Ganina could have matched him, but she was bound to a small child and a band of foreigners not deeply concerned by the fate of her camp. They rode at their own pace, but she knew Caln would carry word to Ifelsten. With that, she must be content.

The land was beautiful, climbing to upland woods and pastures that reminded Ganina of her home. Above her father's camp there had been snow-capped mountains, brooding and majestic, that she still sometimes saw in her dreams. Nothing was that high in Westenia, but it was a bountiful land, full of green grass and abundant water, and as they finally drew close to Shembel the view was magnificent. Farms dotted a rolling landscape stretching far away into purplish hills. She could see silver ribbons outlining their curves and at one point they had to ford a river. For Gilya's sake she stifled her fear, but the Westenians obviously were used to it and crossed without incident.

There were patrols as they neared the temple site, men

who rode up to them for conversation with her party, then turned and cantered rapidly back towards Ifelsten's headquarters. Ganina had thought reaching a source of help would lay her ghosts, but instead they emerged full force. It made everything seem more real, more pressing and urgent, and she began to understand why Caln had been unable to tolerate the slow pace of her party. Now she began to thirst for vengeance, but was not reassured by her conversations with Trebew. He said there had been no sign or word of Senec's troops. Ifelsten might shelter her, but was in no way compelled to fight on her behalf. She could think of him as no more than a host, possibly for much longer than she desired...longer than might be wise.

The temple was lovely and sad—a red sandstone edifice newly rebuilt among gardens only half-redone. This was where the Westenians had made their last, ultimately successful stand against troops sent from Covetia. Ganina remembered the fierce, joyous departure of their fighters from the Camp of the Horsetails and the subsequent return of only a few common soldiers crushed in body and broken in spirit. They had thought Senec was lost. It had been months before he came back with his brother to try to arrange a lasting peace, which Atulfa and Dyak then undermined for two years—until he killed them and made a better one.

"Beautiful, isn't it?" Trebew asked proudly, startling her from her memories.

"Very," she replied politely, unable to tell him she found it unbearably tragic. She had a presentiment that there would be no happiness for her at Shembel.

The people seemed kind, though, when they reached the impressive building where Ifelsten made his home in a hall set apart from the temple. Everything was newly constructed of sandstone that must have been quarried from the surrounding hills. Westenia's chief, formerly a wharf rat if rumors were to be believed, came to greet them, impressively if not richly dressed. Even so, Ganina thought with a flash of amusement, there was something perpetually untidy about the man, as though he could not quite fit within the skin he had grown. He came down the steps with Caln and another blond man, a bodyguard of sorts. From what she had heard, he barely needed one. They said he had been virtually the last man left standing in front of Shembel.

For an uneasy moment, she had the tantalizing sense that only the two of them existed. It was the thing she had felt before, but not so intensely. He looked into her face—fully and caringly, without a need for words in either of their tongues—and reached up for Gilya. The child remembered him and went to him, probably expecting more toys. A woman behind him took Gilya with a smile while Caln spoke to Ganina for the first time.

"May the boy go with one of our ladies? It has been a long ride for him."

Ganina shrugged. "Our children are accustomed to that." She noted him stiffen slightly, understanding that she numbered him with the enemy camp.

"Of course," he said. "All the same, we will care for him. And for you." *Despite your attitude*, his posture said.

"Very well," she agreed, not giving an inch. She would not like this man, no matter that they were now related by marriage. At least with Ifelsten she knew where she stood, but Caln was a traitor. She could not understand why Senec still viewed him with fondness and feared it would be even greater now that they were the only ones left of their mother's blood. There was nothing like death to unite men.

But when Ifelsten offered a hand to help her from her horse, she took it. It was the first time he had touched her and the moment her feet were on the ground, she stepped back. They were close…too close. He released her at once, but not before she had seen a flash of…something…in his eyes.

He offered courtesy, though he had to do it through Caln since he didn't speak her language.

"If you will come with us," Senec's half-brother said with no inflection in his voice, "we will make you comfortable in the hall. The women have prepared quarters for you and the child. You may be with us for some time, depending upon how quickly my brother can crush the Sowetians. My chief hopes that he may return before winter."

She knew Caln's air of frozen watchfulness concealed a swirling whirlpool of rage. For a moment, sympathy overrode her distaste. "I understand how badly you want justice for your kin," she told him. "I, too, have people to avenge." Yes, Donleth, who had saved her life. Little Aben. A few others. Some of them had been cruel to her, but no one deserved to die the way they must have gone, not even the vicious little wives. Those had been lucky to escape when they had but, looking at Caln, she sensed that luck had run its course. He would slaughter them like pigs, women or not.

He just inclined his head very slightly, not as if he was considering her offer of peace between them. "Please come inside." Ganina saw Ifelsten's assessing glance move between them, comprehending that Caln was not her friend. He looked thoughtful, but only called to one of the women to accompany her.

"Thank you." Ganina risked a slight smile at the Westenian leader. "You are most kind." She left with the woman without waiting to hear if Caln translated for her. She doubted it.

The hall was unlike any building Ganina had ever seen. Raised among tents, she felt stifled by walls that didn't move with the wind. It was impressive—a long rectangular building divided by partitions, but open overall to traffic and the conduct of business. No guards were visible. There were some solid walls at the back of the building and the woman with her took her through a door such as she had seen at the guard post, but much bigger. Everything was big, including the quarters into which she was shown.

She could not help breaking into laughter. Inside, Gilya had been shown to a mountain of stuffed cushions among which he was leaping gleefully. The woman with her, a plain-faced red-haired woman she thought was probably a servant, started to giggle.

"Oh, Gilya," Ganina chuckled, "I do not think they are for play."

His only answer was a scream of joy as he flopped belly-down into their softness. "I do, I do!" he shrieked in the age-old fashion of children everywhere, and she found she was unable to stop him for the sake of propriety. He was simply too funny.

Leaving them to their play, the serving-girl moved efficiently around their temporary lodging, pouring water, laying out clothing, bringing in bread and fruit and watered wine for Ganina...juice for Gilya. She gave Ganina a questioning look and spoke a few words ending with an upward lilt. It was recognizably, "Is there anything more?" and Ganina just shook her head, smiling. She would have to learn at least a little Westenian if she was to remain with these people for a time. It might be nice to be able to speak directly to Ifelsten—a small courtesy she could give him. The girl departed, closing the door. Used to the soft fall of a tent flap, Ganina jumped at the sound, feeling inexplicably trapped.

"Gilya, come and eat," she instructed. She did not have to ask twice, but for her part she could only nibble, too uneasy to feel much appetite. There were windows in the hall, shuttered windows. She had never seen anything like them, but they made her feel unbearably closed in. There was a coal stove with a pipe that led to the outside; it gave her a fear of fire she had never felt in her tent. The Westenians had spared nothing for her comfort: a luxurious bed with furs and more pillows took up most of the room, and there was a little alcove with a cot for Gilya. Seeing a closed door to one side of the room, she could not resist padding softly to the door to open it. On the other side lay a dressing room with chairs, a soft small couch and basins for washing. There were three rooms for just the two of them, generous by any estimation, and she already knew spacious grounds and gardens lay outside. They would be comfortable, but for how long? How long must she live with only the memory of her dead, among people with whom she shared nothing? When would Senec come? She prayed it would be soon. For many reasons, she needed him to come quickly.

When Gilya had eaten and napped she took him outside to find a privy, and she had lived for too many years in camps often bound for war not to know this looked like one. Perhaps she had been wrong about Ifelsten not fighting for her. Long lines of horses were being trotted in from pasture by shouting, bustling men. As she and Gilya watched, they saw distant figures of more men pouring oil atop a large beacon set on a high hillock. Descending to the ground, they fired flame arrows into the prepared faggots, which erupted in a message visible to all. Either war had come to Westenia or Westenia was going to war.

Caln had to tell her, since he was one of the few who could. Passing, he saw her standing indecisively with the child. Her lost expression apparently touched something in him, because he paused in mid-stride and doubled back.

"We now have enemies on our border," he told her. "Your clan is dead. Without their influence and with Senec gone, Illinea's and Drusa's tribes will take over. They did not sign the compact. Therefore, we are still at war with them. We cannot wait until the autumn for Senec to return. They will have gained too much power by then."

"I see. What about your wife and children?" Ganina wondered.

"They have been without me before."

"Will you take lightning fire into my land again?" she asked, scornfully.

"If we must. It will not be used against anyone who is peaceful."

"Then I hope the fathers have not yet aroused too many."

Caln had threaded the beads of war into his hair; the man who had betrayed Covetians still shared their customs. She found him bizarre. He no longer wore his hair long enough to knot it, but otherwise his appearance was a blend of cultures, with leather leggings and boots appropriate to Juragia, Covetian warbeads, and a good Westenian broadsword strapped to his hip. No doubt he would carry one of the Covetian bows when he departed for her land. He looked as taut and lethal as one, primed and ready for the kill, eyes glowing with barely-repressed violence.

"When do you leave?" she asked.

"Not until morning." She heard regret in his voice. He had had nine half-brothers and sisters in the camp. For him, this war would not be political, but personal. It would be Caln, not Senec, who would blot the camps of the offenders from the face of the earth. Even in this, her husband would be robbed.

"There are a few here who speak some Covetian," Caln went on. "Try to learn Westenian from them. You will need it. It is possible Senec may reach our port city before we return, so if he sends riders here for you, go. You will be kept safe until then."

Safe and in the dark, Ganina thought. He was right. She must learn the language…the people. It had been the furthest thing from her mind, but she must make friends of her enemies.

"Go with luck," she said, "and without mercy." It was what one said to a Covetian departing for war.

"If you see my brother first, tell him he will be avenged," he acknowledged it.

She was sure of that. Her brother-in-law was a handsome man, even desirable. He had parted from his wife and children with unfeigned tenderness…even the child that was not his. Yet she had seen that look on him she associated with Atulfa and

Senec and knew the tribes of her husband's former wives were about to pay a terrible price. Without Gilya in their possession, they had no shield. They must know it, too. It would be like waiting for the hand of death to drag them into the abyss.

"What about Senec's daughters?" To Westenians, those children would be indistinguishable from all the others.

"They will die. It is what their grandfathers risked."

The stark and bitter truth rose up in Ganina like gall. She had sat on one council of peace because Senec had given her a break from serving. He had given her clothes and jewelry and servants to placate her, and she had deluded herself that he had given her responsibilities when he departed. Yes, she had been empowered to sit in simple judgment, to move the camp if she felt it necessary, but that was nothing. The power of life and death lay with men. It always had; it always would. Life really had little value, after all. The women of the tribe were expected to replenish it because men squandered it so readily. But she put a polite expression on the face that bade farewell to her brother-in-law. It was what women did.

* * * *

At dawn the troops departed, every man mounted. There were no foot soldiers among the Westenians; in that way they were like the Covetians. Some of the nations they had subjugated had tried fighting Covetia with troops on foot and had perished almost to a man. Nothing could stand against cavalry, especially when it bore the dreaded lightning fire Ganina knew must be on the pack animals of the Westenians.

She rose early and took the child with her to bid them farewell, noting at once—as a woman accustomed to the ways of war—that Ifelsten and Caln co-led the men. Everyone knew they had done it at the battle of Shembel and that they had proven unbeatable. It appeared from the ease with which they dealt with one another that there was a deep bond of friendship between them. Probably, Ganina thought, it was because Caln wanted nothing that Ifelsten possessed. A chief could risk friendship only with such men and they were rare. But what of Ifelsten's heart? Why had he not given that to any woman? Of course, he had a checkered past.

There was no sign of the bar-room brawler in Ifelsten that morning. Ganina had heard Senec's men talk of him in tones of grudging respect. They said that despite mongrel breeding he was a leader of men and he looked it that day—still vaguely untidy, but dressed, armed and armored for war, riding the gray horse Senec had given him. It was easily visible to the troops, who joked and jostled in the way of men setting out for bloodshed. She wondered if it was how they defied death.

But Ifelsten was serious and when he began to address the troops, the men quieted instantly. Ganina understood nothing and thought she would be left in ignorance. Ifelsten had not forgotten her presence, though, or the fact that she had raised the alarm of trouble on his border. He sent her mysterious brother-in-law with a message.

"I salute your courage," Caln spoke the words for him, impassively. "And you have my promise of revenge for the lives of your people. If you see your husband before I do, tell him for me."

"I will," she replied, meeting Ifelsten's level blue gaze across the crowd. There was no taint of drink on him. He was clear-eyed and steady, his large hands strong and capable on the reins. She remembered the feel of them with something between dread and arousal. It was so dangerous to feel desire for a man other than her husband, yet she felt a singing in her bones despite everything. She could not even speak to the Westenian chief directly. Why should she feel such attraction to him...such assurance that he shared it? It was preposterous, a perilous fantasy she must expunge from her mind. So she presented to him the same cool expression she had shown to Caln the previous day, wishing a formal goodbye to the only man with whom she would have ridden into war.

Chapter Fourteen

In the gloom of half-evening, Ganina sat with the serving girl, Calill, before a coal fire to which she could not accustom herself. The dim light was not to her liking...nor the change of seasons it portended...nor the fact that both men—Senec and Ifelsten—remained away. No news came from Senec and scarcely more from Ifelsten.

She had busied herself in every possible way, spending long hours outdoors with Gilya when the weather was good. But inevitably he made friends and had less need of her, and she had no ability to speak with the mothers of those children, at least not until Pytor the Priest began teaching her Westenian. He had been a real friend, as had Calill, who was busy passing her tiny cakes topped with beaten butter and honey that they always ate with hot mint tea.

"In my camp," Ganina reflected, "we would have been happy with cold tea and goat cheese smeared on bread. You live well. Your land is rich, your pastures lush. Never have I seen orchards so heavy-bearing." She smiled sardonically. "So long as you are not invaded by Covetians."

"Yes." Calill poured tea for her erstwhile mistress. "That is why our chief made haste to the border."

"It is self-interest," Ganina mused. She must not think of it in any other way or that a man other than her husband was avenging her loss. Must not feel that a kind and humorous man who inspired loyalty in his troops might do the same for her, more so than her husband's distant concern. She had no right to think such things.

"I hope all of the men return before snow falls." Calill sounded carefully neutral. "Does it snow in Covetia?" She spoke slowly so that Ganina could understand her, but generally they had little difficulty understanding one another. To Ganina's surprise, some words in their languages were similar. The enmity between their lands had run so deep, it was easy to forget they had shared a border time out of mind. More than the occasional errant traveler had crossed that line.

"In the north, where I come from. Not often in the south, though the wind can be bitter in winter. Senec was going to move to the lowlands for the cold season this year."

The other woman gave her a look of sympathy. "It will never be the same, I know, but when your men return, they will make another camp."

"Yes." Ganina did not like to think of the future and would not encourage thoughts of the past. There was only the idle present, drinking tea.

An abrupt knock at the outer door made her jump. Accustomed to someone simply calling for entrance, she had been unable to adjust to the Westenian custom, but she had learned Pytor's knock and called, "Come."

The young man entered on a gush of cool air scented by smoke and apples. Cider was being pressed; its pungent smell hung over the grounds like a memory of summer. Ganina smiled at him with genuine fondness. He was a far cry from the middle-aged or elderly Covetian priests—different in every way. Modest and self-effacing, Pytor had no direct political involvement and did not seek any, as far as she could tell. Her own priests were men of such importance that their tentacles wound through every camp in Covetia. Even the fathers of her enemies would not dare kill one. Priests were bound to be the only people still living near the Camp of the Horsetails.

"Good news!" Pytor smiled broadly. "Our troops return. An advance rider has just reached us. They will arrive within the week."

"Thank Franta, god of fortune," Calill said piously, but Ganina was rendered speechless for a moment. Bitterly disappointed it was not word of her husband, still she was conscious of a guilty underlying excitement to know that Ifelsten's men returned…that he returned alive and well.

"That is very good news," she forced herself to say, politely. "Still no word of Covetian troops?"

"No, Lady. They are probably delayed by rough seas at this time of year. It is not easy crossing into our port once summer has passed."

"I see." No one had explained this to her, but it made sense. Her people were not sailors and if they had killed too many of the Sowetians who were, they would have difficulty assembling a crew. The returning Westenians rode fine long-legged horses that could make good speed as long as snow was not yet falling.

"There were casualties." Pytor signed himself to whatever god protected souls. "But all in all, it was not a hard campaign, I gather."

"Again, good news." She was carefully politic. No matter that they had gone to destroy her enemies, Ifelsten's troops still had invaded her land and it gave her a queasy feeling. Fortunately, Gilya chose that moment to dart back through the door Pytor had just closed, admitting a blast as he streaked for her lap, climbing like a wood squirrel to throw his arms around her neck. He smelled like a vat of something brewing.

"Mama, Mama," he exulted, making her wince. His mother was dead, of that much she was certain. "They're coming back. Soldiers on BIG horses!"

"I know." She smiled guiltily at the little boy so readily accepting her. She had never asked that he call her Mama, but six months was a long time in the life of such a small child. She wondered how much he remembered of his mother, though she never asked that either, reluctant to interfere with his settling-in. "I know they are, Gilya." She smiled at the priest over the head of the child. "Soon you will see your friend Ifelsten again."

* * * *

At twilight on the fifth day, the Hall was alive with energy, for the men were expected. Ganina had left her rooms, drinking hot cider with the others before the huge hearth in the outer chambers. The bite in the air made any warm beverage welcome and she thought with a pang of the sufferings Senec and his men must be enduring on a cold winter sea, assuming they had gotten that far. No one had thought the Sowetians could present serious opposition. Then again, she reminded herself, they had made that mistake about Westenia, too…as a result of which she sat among her former enemies, a refugee from her own land. War was a most curious business.

Stretching her toes surreptitiously towards the fire, she looked at the sea of faces in the room. Westenian, every one. But she had begun to know them, from Calill who served her cheerfully…to Pytor…to Sinia the laundress…to the mothers of Gilya's playmates. There was Orneck, captain of the Hall Guard, a sharp-eyed veteran who nonetheless had been warm to her. For just a few hours longer, she thought, these people could shield her from the terrible reality returning with Ifelsten and his men. Flame chuckled merrily up the massive stone chimney and a smell of apples and frost and baking bread hung in the air. Chatter she could now understand flowed around her like a warm pool of comfort.

When, she wondered, had she begun to feel so at home with these people? But this was not her home. As soon as her husband returned, she would be bound for Covetia to do...what? How could they begin again? Selfishly, she clung to the warm drink in her hand and smiles on the faces of people around her. Soon, those would be only memories. Grief clutched at her briefly before she thrust away its presence, steeling herself as the massive main door opened to admit Orneck. The smile below his fierce blonde mustache said everything.

"They are coming," he announced. At once, there were outcries and thanks uttered to the gods as a massive tide of humanity flowed towards that door. She rose, calling Gilya to her, surprised to feel Pytor touch her elbow. His handsome face was creased with concern. He alone, she thought, gave consideration to the grief she was about to suffer rather than his own joy. It was what set him apart.

"Calill," he summoned the serving girl, who looked to be on the edge of flight. "Fetch a warm cloak for Lady Ganina, and one for yourself."

"Of course," the girl murmured, abashed. She disappeared momentarily into the apartments at the end of the Hall, then returned with a hooded gray wool cloak to go over the loose amethyst-colored gown Ganina wore, Westenian-style. Every stitch she and Gilya wore had been given them by their enemies.

Swathing the protesting child in the voluminous folds of her cloak, she turned to Pytor, jaw set.

"Hush," she told Gilya with uncharacteristic firmness. "We're going right now." Bearing the precious burden of his squirming weight on her hip, with his head peeking from the cloth like the face of a little squirrel, she took a deep breath and started for the door with Pytor beside her.

The men had broken out torches to relieve the gloom. Against their flicker and sputter, she saw the unmistakable outline of Ifelsten's gray stallion emerge from the first fall of snow, accompanied by two outriders and a familiar black pony. Ganina strained for a better view, disbelieving. Someone must have told him she wanted her pony and the ruler of Westenia was bringing him back to her.

Clad in a bright scarlet cloak, Ifelsten wore nothing on his head, the better for people to see him. And see him they did, clapping and cheering as he rode in smiling, hair and beard lightly coated with white.

He saw her at once. His eyes settled on hers. The moment was broken by Gilya's firm kick on her hip, painful enough that she let him slide from beneath her cloak. His booted feet left tiny tracks as he ran unerringly towards the man who had made him toy horses. Ganina had kept the memory alive for him, but regretted it as she saw the child dart among horses abruptly reined in by their riders. She held her breath, but Covetian children had no fear of horses, which were some of their first nursemaids. In many households, ponies were kept right inside the tents. Or they had been, Ganina amended. There were no more tents, only the solid Hall behind her and the graceful outline of the Temple of Shembel, where new snow sprinkled the gardens and summer-fat carp dwelt at the bottom of their pond awaiting spring.

"Halloo," Ifelsten greeted Gilya, his booming voice recognizable even among the noise of the crowd. He had dismounted and bent down, picking up the little boy without hesitation, nuzzling him and laughing. "Little man, you have grown."

"I am BIG," Gilya asserted with his customary boldness, and Ifelsten laughed again.

"You are." Holding the child braced against his chest with one arm, Westenia's chief turned to the assembled crowd. It was a surreal moment for Ganina, watching the man who had destroyed her enemies holding what was essentially her child, in place of his father. It was Ifelsten who would be the child's hero, Ifelsten to whom he would run looking for tenderness and toys. If Senec did not return soon, it was even possible he would forget him as he had forgotten his mother. But just then, Ifelsten motioned for silence with his free hand. The dull roar muted.

"We return to you triumphant," he assured them. "Our borders are secure. The camps of those warlords who did not sign our treaty are gone, never to rise again. The priests have vowed to us they will hold the peace until their leader returns. Your men have defended you well. Some have perished. Word will be brought to the families by troop leaders."

The crowd was utterly silent then, their jubilation extinguished like a candle snuffed out. Already Ganina could see the strained faces of anxious women searching among the men. This would not be a triumph for everyone.

"In the lowlands where we have taken territory," Ifelsten went on, shushing Gilya, "an honored place has been given to the fallen. Their graves are marked, every one, for their kin. In the spring, we will make pilgrimage with their families. In the meantime, widows and parents may apply through their commanding officers for a pension. Have word sent through the officers if anyone is in need of housing or help. We cannot replace your loved ones, but we can show our gratitude."

A murmur ran through the crowd and he gave them a small, appropriately subdued smile. "Now our men will go to the Hall for food and rest. You may join us there." Ganina knew the cooks were prepared for an onslaught; they had been baking since the dark hours of the morning.

He turned aside and the crowd broke, with families streaming towards men. Couples embraced; sounds of crying and the laughter of children filled the encroaching night, along with the punctuating snorts of horses. Frost-rimed steam rose from their nostrils and there was a pungent smell of manure and urine as some relieved themselves in the manner of animals returning to their home stables. A few unsecured dogs gamboled among the crowd, many of them leaping on men who belonged to them.

But none of those men were hers, not even the one who wished to be.

Chapter Fifteen

Ifelsten came up the steps of the Hall with the little boy securely in his grasp, but swung him down and set him on his feet. When he smiled at her, Ganina saw that his eyes were very blue by the light of flaring torches. Droplets of melting snow clung to his honey-colored beard. He exuded the smell of horse and the less pleasing odor of wet wool.

"My lord, you should come in," she said. "You are wet and cold."

His face betrayed a mixture of pleasure and surprise.

"You have learned Westenian."

"A little."

"Go in, go in!" Gilya abetted her plan by crowing and gamboling about them and Pytor like a frolicsome colt. They headed a phalanx of people making for delicacies set out on long tables at one side of the huge Hall.

"It's a good thing." Ifelsten ushered her courteously through the broad doorway. "Caln returned home." He frowned at the noise inside. "We will never hear each other this way, though. Come to my apartments."

Unasked, Pytor accompanied them, and Ganina gave him a sharp sideways look. His expression was bland, but she had the sudden conviction that he knew of the attraction between her and Ifelsten and had positioned himself as a chaperone. It was both a disappointment and a relief. Gilya clamored for food until Ganina relented and let him go. Calill would watch the child, so the three adults went directly to Ifelsten's apartments, which lay at the opposite end from Ganina's. Like hers, they were enclosed. But when they entered, she saw that they were much more sumptuous…not rich, precisely, but everything was of the finest materials. His wall hangings and coverlets had been carefully crafted by women who knew their business; the furniture was comfortable, the draperies and rugs thick and rich. A generous fire burned on the main hearth where he took her; he apparently preferred a traditional wood fire like the one in the main hall, although others used coal. One woman appeared to bring them food and drink, while another took his cloak and its ornate brooch. But after that, he sat on a well-padded divan to pull off his own boots, throwing them unceremoniously in a corner.

"Long ride." He stretched and groaned. No kingly man, this one. He had the robust body of a workman, clearly outlined by his homespun tunic and leather trousers. She could easily envision him settling down to a meal of sausage and ale in some waterfront tavern. But he had thought first of an anxious guest rather than of his own people waiting to celebrate. That was a kingly gesture. And to bring the pony…she could hardly conceive of such kindness.

The dinner was grand: beef and ham and capon, white bread, cheese and relishes and sweetmeats. And wine and mead—plenty of it. Ganina already knew Ifelsten was a man who liked his spirits. He ate like he was famished, mumbling around his meal in a way that strained her limited capacity to understand Westenian.

"Caln's home lies between Covetia and Shembel," he reminded her, "so he stayed behind to tend his farm." She remembered her night and morning spent there with the silent little wife who had never uttered a word beyond one command to the dog. How did they manage? But judging by the number of children they had, they did. The little girl had spoken in good Covetian, but she was shy. Ganina had learned very little from that one…certainly not who her father was. Not why Caln lived between two worlds or why he had betrayed them.

"But I don't think we'll need him to translate," Ifelsten continued.

He was eating heartily while Ganina, on edge, merely picked at the feast. Whatever news he brought would not be good, even if it was news of revenge.

"We found what was left of your camp," he finally said, swigging wine. He wiped his lips on his slightly frayed tunic sleeve without apology, as if accustomed to doing it. "The raiders just took what they wanted and left." He frowned. "They had brought all the bodies into the open, so they more or less had sky burial. We found bones, mostly.

"Caln went to your priests, who gave them proper burial. Then we rode north. They had made straight for their camps, trying to fortify them. When the men chasing you didn't come back, they must have known what was going to happen, but I think they were expecting Senec. They thought they had more time.

"We tracked them for a month," he said after another enormous swallow of wine. Ganina knew her brain would explode if she ever tried a trick like that. "They were in the camps with their women and children." He shook his head, which appeared unaffected. "Since it was Caln's kin who were murdered, I let him lead the charge. The men love him, you know. He saved all our asses at the battle here and they haven't forgotten. They knew they were avenging him and they killed...everything. Senec's daughters were probably among them, I'm sorry to say. It was impossible to tell who was who, except Caln said they had a number of men from the borderlands in the camps. A surprising number."

Ganina had roughly comprehended most of what he said and nodded. Between the middle warlords and her father's men in the north lay a broad expanse of trackless waste, sandstone canyons and caves in which leaderless men had always taken refuge. Fiercely independent and bound to no one, they were equally feared in both north and south, yet apparently for some reason they had thrown in with Illinea's and Drusa's fathers. She supposed they, like everyone else, had been impoverished by the war and made desperate. And what riches existed in Covetia were thought to lie with Senec.

"I'm sorry," Ifelsten repeated. "We leveled those camps as if they had never existed and then rode to your head priest, Jaric. He agreed to send messages to all the other camps telling them that as long as they keep the peace, they are safe from us."

"With Senec gone," Ganina agreed, "he is the one they will listen to."

"That was what Caln told me. I know that you don't like him, Ganina, but he is invaluable in dealing with your country. Going to the priests undoubtedly saved many lives and it will hold things together for Senec."

She felt Pytor gently lift one of her hands, squeezing in a gesture of support. It was the only thing that felt real—that and the heat of the roaring fire. Her bones were cold despite it, with a chill that reached all the way to her heart.

"Hold it together for what?" she murmured. "I am sorry." She rose abruptly. "I must be alone."

Ifelsten turned to the priest. "Will you see the Lady back to her apartments?"

"Of course."

In a haze, she let Pytor guide her back to the only home she had as of that moment. In Covetia, there would be nothing but empty land stretching away to the horizon, reminding her of tents that had dotted it and people whose voices were stilled forever. All at once, she wanted very badly to crawl into her comfortable bed and not rise again. She needed company there, needed her husband's arms around her…his support. Granted that he could be chilly at times, nevertheless she had felt safe with him. Where was he? Why did he not come? Not bothering to change, she tumbled into her lonely bed. Outside, festivities proceeded without her. Though they might not think of it in that light, those people were celebrating the deaths of Senec's little daughters. For the first time she cried, but eventually the blessed oblivion of sleep claimed her.

* * * *

Things looked no better in the morning…only whiter. The first snow had fallen, good for the children to run screaming and skidding about the great brooding Temple of Shembel, sitting shrouded in wrecked majesty. From the doorway where she sent Gilya out to play, Ganina could see Pytor prowling among its columns as though trying to commune with it, and she went down the steps with warmed bread and honey.

"Do you always do that?" he asked, accepting it.

"Do what?"

"Serve people. You could have sent Calill."

She shrugged, suddenly diffident, unsure if it was criticism. "It is just my way. I was not always Senec's wife. When

I was married to his father, I was only the youngest of many wives and expected to see to his every whim." She could not help smiling ruefully. "He had many."

"Were you fond of him?"

"Atulfa?" She shook her head. "No one was fond of Atulfa, not even Senec. Atulfa ruled through fear. People feared Senec, too, but they always knew he would look out for them." She stared into the distance, jaw working. "And he did, until he left for Sowetia. I fear he grew overconfident. He had bribed his wives' fathers handsomely and thought that was enough, even when they refused to sign the treaty. Instead, they wanted more." She gestured toward Gilya, romping happily in the snow, oblivious of the fate that had awaited him. "They would have taken his son for blackmail. Gilya is the reason they came to our camp."

"Well, you put a stop to that."

"At great cost to the others, yes."

"Oh, come, Ganina. Surely you don't think they would have let anyone live? You did for Senec and his men the only thing you could do—saved his son, at great risk to your own life. Now you hold his country for him. This has purged your land of a festering mass which would have threatened us eventually."

"Senec could have dealt with it, with my father's help," Ganina speculated. "But instead he chose to go to Sowetia." Her tone was aggrieved despite her resolve not to criticize her husband.

"He needed money," Pytor pointed out. "Badly. They had cut off their tribute for too long, Ganina; he had to have it. He can no longer get anything from the lands closest to yours. We and the Juragians have lightning fire and will force him to keep the peace, so he had no choice but to go far afield for gold. Frankly, no one cares what he does there."

"But what if they also get the fire?"

"Ah, smart girl," he complimented, tapping her forehead gently. "Yes, eventually all will get it and then many things will change. Each leader knows this and struggles to put his land in the strongest possible position. Senec has ambitions far beyond being warlord of your camp. He would be lord of all the camps—all the land. I think if he had to sacrifice one camp in that interest, he would do it, though it will grieve him."

"Grieve him? It may destroy him." She shivered again, not entirely from cold. "You do not understand our ways. Many a warlord confronted with such devastation and bearing the burden of it would simply ride into the hills, never to be seen again. I fear that he may choose that fate once we return to Covetia."

"He will have to choose between the old ways and the new," the priest said, with a toughness that surprised her. "He must be a leader of men or not. But he has always gone with the new. That is why he and Ifelsten get along well. Besides, there is no one else to raise his son, unless he gives him to Caln."

"No!" Ganina protested at once. "Gilya is mine!"

"But he is not," Pytor argued shrewdly. "He is no blood kin to you, but he is to Caln and Caln would always take another child."

"As he took his wife's daughter?" Ganina guessed.

"Yes." Pytor looked at her curiously. "Has no one told you about Delfi? She was our own, a priestess of Shembel, grievously assaulted by your soldiers. She bore a child by one of them and gave it up to a Covetian family, but they perished at the hands of our soldiers and she took her daughter back. Ironic, isn't it?"

"It is terrible. Did she lose her reason?"

"Only her speech. She can speak a little if she is not nervous or afraid. But she was beaten so badly that she had no memory of who she was, and no speech to ask. Caln did not know. He took her in out of charity."

"And a good deal more," Ganina corrected tartly, remembering the two children who looked like him.

"Of course there is more," Pytor agreed. "They have a deep love between them. Even when Ifelsten offered Caln the governorship of our new territory he would not take it, because he knew it would be too hard for Delfi. He could be a rich man, but he turns the soil like any farmer. Except when we need him, of course, and then his neighbors do it."

"He did that for his wife?" Ganina marveled. "He is not as Covetian as I thought."

"It influences him, but he is other things as well and his life is here. Try not to think too harshly of him. He is your family now, after all."

"I have not spoken to him of my feelings," Ganina replied, somewhat stiffly.

"Well, he feels them," Pytor said. "He is not stupid or insensitive, you know. For your husband's sake, try to manage with him. They were always close and now they have only each other."

"Senec has me." Even as she said it, Ganina knew how ridiculous that was. To a Covetian man, his woman was a receptacle for his lust and the means through which children were obtained. If he happened to feel some liking for her into the bargain that was fortunate, but it wasn't necessary or expected.

But either Pytor did not know that or he was being kind. "Yes, he is lucky," he said with a smile.

"Well, until he comes, I must bide as best I am able," Ganina decided aloud. "Today I will cut new clothes for Gilya. Tomorrow…who knows? Show him how to make snowballs, I suppose."

"He already knows. He hit me twice."

Finally, she could smile. "Does he have a good arm?"

"For a three-year-old."

Chapter Sixteen

As the tent flap parted, wind carried in a sharp scent of frosty pine needles soon to crystallize with ice. Stirred by the cold, Senec rolled towards the opening. There was a time when he would never have slept with his back to any entrance, but it was Kaleel entering. No one else had attended him for many days, so that the troops remained largely ignorant of Senec's condition since Ifelsten's messenger had delivered his disastrous news.

"How're the ribs?"

"Still broken." Senec propped himself up in his bedroll far enough to accept a mug of chica from Ganina's father. Every milk cow in the area had been turned into meat and the barley sugar was long since gone, so nothing remained but hot, bitter brew. It was better than nothing.

"They will be for another month," Kaleel pointed out. "We can't sit here that long."

"No one asked you to."

The older man raised one grizzled brow. The other, intersected by a sword-scar, gave him a permanently quizzical, faintly contemptuous look. "You propose we leave you?"

"I can ride."

"Then I will tell the men to break camp in the morning."

"I will tell them."

"When?"

Senec made an impatient gesture. "When I'm ready."

There was nothing in the tent for him to sit on and only a small fire crackling with a muted sound, so Kaleel rocked back on his heels before it, waiting with the air of a man accustomed to scant comforts. "Our firewood is running out and we have only enough provisions to reach the city. We can't lay siege if they defend it."

Senec merely grimaced above his mug. "My father took that city twice. They open the gates because they know no one will wreck a seaport and they'd rather live."

Kaleel nodded thoughtfully. A mountain chieftain, he had lacked battle experience in Sowetia, though not elsewhere. But Senec had accompanied Atulfa on several lengthy campaigns there, so in the past months it was his lead that taken them the length of Sowetia to its southern port. They had laid waste to everything in their path and acquired substantial booty, but apparently the glut of destruction was nearing an end.

"We will waste no time putting out to sea," Senec went on. "My troops will make for the harbor. The Sowetian fleet will be holed up there, but we still have time to sail across to Westenia. Take what stores you will, impress men, meet us and get horses aboard. Then we go straight to Shembel."

"Agreed." Though Kaleel only let his gaze run fleetingly

across Senec's bandaged chest, the younger man read his thoughts as clearly as if he had spoken.

"I can ride," Senec repeated. "I'm well strapped and once I'm aboard ship it's not a factor." Privately, Senec had no illusions about the discomforts of a pre-winter sail across seas which would be choppy at best. A good gale could kill him. But to Kaleel he showed a face of indifference.

"True." The other chieftain merely continued sipping, his expression inscrutable as well. A heavy red-gold beard largely concealed Kaleel's features. His resemblance to Ganina would have been more noticeable but for the scar across his sightless eye. Otherwise he was fit and had led the troops capably when Senec was thrown down nearly the entirety of a cliff in pitched battle. He had hauled him up by rope, too, when he could have let him fall and taken command, so on the whole Senec was inclined to trust his father-in-law as much as was wise. By all accounts Ganina had also acquitted herself honorably, with more courage than one expected of a woman. Possibly he had made a more fortunate marriage this time.

Nothing could have proven less fortunate than the previous two, but he could not think of that now. If he did, he might well go mad. Messengers had reached him to tell him he was being avenged and he knew Caln's men would have blotted out his five little daughters without even knowing who they were. But that was then. Now was now. Or at least so he must tell himself.

"We will take Ganina and Gilya and return at speed to Covetia," he instructed. "I have the priests to deal with."

"Send their share of gold ahead," Kaleel suggested. "Just not all of it."

Senec permitted himself a faint smile. "They might have earned it this time."

"Act quickly, or you will never get them out of power."

"I know." Senec did not take offense at his father-in-law's cautionary tone, for if the priests had grown too comfortable governing in his stead, it could prove difficult to dislodge them. He no longer had warriors other than those who traveled with him—and Kaleel's men. Having lost three camps, he could not make another misstep. Even his father had not dealt so disastrously with the people.

But he had a son. And Ifelsten had his wife. He didn't trust Westenia's leader to resist his attraction to her indefinitely, and since he needed Ifelsten as an ally, it would be most unfortunate if he had to return to Shembel only to murder the man. He must reclaim his kin as quickly as possible.

He stood up without the grunt of pain he would have liked to utter. The cold air on his chest made his broken ribs ache disastrously, but he merely pulled on a doublet, hooded fur cloak and mitts without showing any sign of weakness. He already wore boots and heavy pantaloons, grateful for his wife's foresight in sending them with him on his first journey away from her. Now her father stood, watching expectantly as he readied himself to appear before the men and show them he had not lost his wits though he might be in disgrace. It would be a long journey back in many ways.

Chapter Seventeen

This time no runner appeared to warn Ifelsten that his ally of the moment was approaching. The Covetians had no men to spare. That was why from inside her rooms Ganina heard running footsteps and people shouting. A column approaching without warning could be anyone.

But it was not anyone. Craning her neck for a view of snow-shrouded riders as she stood with everyone else in front of the hall, she cursed volubly. Pytor was visibly shocked, as if he had never suspected she knew those words.

"My father," she said bitterly, earning another shocked look. "Whom I never wished to see again."

Kaleel rode at the head of the column because he could; Senec did not because he couldn't. Carried in a blanket between two horses, he entered Shembel not only in disgrace but in a sling.

"The gods," Ganina uttered—now quietly—when she finally figured out where he was. He would have tied himself to his horse, unless he was dying. She ran down the steps and straight past her father without a word, to the makeshift litter. Although she couldn't see who was in it, she knew Senec's distinctive piebald horse, and he was being led, bearing one side of the sling. There was only one person it could be.

They had shrouded him in blankets against the falling snow and for a moment she thought possibly he was dead, but no one stopped her as she lifted back a corner of one blanket. Not dead, then. Senec squinted up at her through flakes drifting down, said her name, and then closed his eyes again.

Men were swarming around her then—Ifelsten's men. He had known when he saw her run to the litter where Senec was and responded at once. The Westenians had long experience dealing with the wounded and traded off expertly with the Covetian riders, working poles through the sides of the blanket to lift her husband free.

"Take him to my quarters," she instructed, asserting privilege. But it was the logical spot and no one argued. She noted in passing that Ifelsten was standing beside her father's horse, both of them heavily engaged in conversation with the aid of someone who understood them. But she was busy directing the men carrying Senec to her rooms, with Pytor hurrying beside her. He had attended their wounded many times.

"Roll him on his side," he told the men. "Carefully. Now roll the blankets up to his back. Good. Roll him back the other way. Now pull."

They extricated Senec like a caterpillar out of its cocoon, but he had not stirred. Behind her, Ganina heard heavy booted footsteps and look up from her husband only long enough to see her father with Ifelsten.

"What happened?" she demanded.

It was her father who answered. "He took a fall down a cliff while we were still in Sowetia. Broke himself up pretty badly and then we had the long sail back here. I think it finished breaking whatever wasn't already broken."

"Get him warm," Pytor said shortly. "I need the medicines from my chamber." Serving girls standing in the doorway scattered to do his bidding. "And warm some baking stones. We will pack him."

Ganina was on her knees beside her bed by then, so alarmed that she did not even question where Gilya was. She only hoped he had not seen this.

"Can I touch him?" she asked anxiously.

"Only his head," Pytor replied. "I think the damage is elsewhere."

No one questioned his judgment in such cases. Their priests had trained him well before the Covetians slaughtered them. Now he was all they had.

Two girls rushed in with the items Pytor had specified. He took a knife from among them and began carefully cutting away Senec's clothes and the bandages swathing his ribs. Behind her, Ganina heard Ifelsten ordering everyone else out, then closing the door. At last she was more or less alone with her husband, save for her father and Ifelsten, Pytor and a girl waiting with warmed stones wrapped in flannel. Ifelsten was the one to think of building up the fire and did so, silently. There was no sound in the room except the chink of new coals catching as he piled them on top.

"How long has he been like this?" Pytor asked.

"Since the port," her father said.

It was a substantial ride from their port at Asteros. Ganina smoothed back Senec's hair, noting that it was damp, and was wracked with pity. It had to have been a deeply painful journey. Small wonder that he was now only semi-conscious.

"Can we give him opa juice?" she asked Pytor, who nodded.

"Nothing to lose, I think," he responded. "Go ahead. Don't choke him."

Choking with broken ribs could prove fatal, so Ganina meted out juice from Pytor's supply with the greatest care. She, too, had nursed wounded and injured men and well knew its use.

"Come, Senec," she whispered to her husband, raising his head fractionally. "Try to drink this."

Saying nothing, he swallowed. He looked visibly thinner, with eyes deeply shadowed, and utterly spent. She thought he probably heard her but was simply too exhausted to respond. Laying his head down gently, she put a hand on his chest not low enough to harm his ribs but high enough to feel his heartbeat. It still beat rhythmically, not faltering.

"His heart is good," she said hopefully, and Pytor nodded.

He was examining his patient carefully, looking at every injury. Those mainly consisted of bruises. But bruises meant damage beneath. Everyone else in the room was silent, as if holding their breath might mean Senec would live. Ganina felt someone squeeze her shoulder, from above, whether her father or Ifelsten she could not have said. But if she had, she would have guessed Ifelsten.

It was Kaleel who spoke, however. "He is a good fighter, your husband."

Her father had never been generous with praise. This was as close as he came. She just nodded, silently.

At last Pytor had finished. He beckoned to the girl, who adroitly packed the warmed stones around Senec, working as if she had done it before.

"You can cover him," Pytor said, and Ganina quickly drew up her warmest comforter, thick with goose down. "The best thing right now is rest."

"There is no more you can do?" she asked, but Pytor shook his head. "Can you wrap his ribs?"

"It would do more harm than good to disturb him. Rest is the best medicine and sometimes the only one. I think this is such a case. He's at the end of his strength."

The thought nearly decimated her. Ganina had never seen Senec anything other than robust and stoic. No one had. This shell of a man was not the husband she remembered nor the leader anyone else did. Such weakness was dangerous in more ways than one. There was no concealing it from the men who had had to carry him in. For the first time, she looked at her father.

"Thank you for saving him."

"Come," Pytor repeated to the men and the girl. "He must rest. We will leave him with Ganina; he will be easiest with her." To her vast relief, they started for the door.

"Just bring me water and oil," she called after the girl. "Warmed. Have the women keep Gilya."

The girl gave a nervous half-nod and filed out with the men. They were already speaking in low tones, about what Ganina did not care. Her job would be to keep her husband alive.

Chapter Eighteen

When the room was warm and she had what she required, she bathed the dirt of battle and travel from Senec as best she could, frowning at what she saw. Ribs she presumed were the ones still whole were plainly visible and he had a lean in-hollowing above the belly he'd not had before. His hip bones were more prominent. He had lost a substantial amount of weight. Bruises still shadowed certain places even a month past his injury. And he never stirred, not until she cupped his manhood in her palm thoughtfully. If he had suffered injury there, Covetia might have no more heirs.

"Not now," he said clearly, and it took her a moment to realize he was joking. Unaccountably, she blushed. She had lain with him dozens of times. There were no secrets between them. Straightening up, she pulled her gown over her head, then the shift beneath it, kicking off her slippers. When she was naked, she lay down carefully beside him, pulling the comforter over them both. She would warm him with her own body.

Unexpectedly, he put one arm around her. She had not thought he had the strength, but she gladly scooted closer to him, laying the side of her face carefully against the shoulder she knew was not broken and her hand over his heart. She saw that his eyes were open, but he was not looking at her, instead staring fixedly at some point in space. It was the place of memory, she thought. She also thought he was entirely in his wits and knew his own weakness and that it probably frightened him.

Gently, she traced the line of his lips through his beard. "Just be still, my love. The priest says you need rest and will be well again."

It was not exactly what Pytor had said. Senec's only response was to turn his face away, though he did not withdraw his arm, and she understood. He did not want her to see him at his most vulnerable. But, of course, she already had.

"Where is Gilya?"

"With the women," she murmured. "He is well, but I did not want him to see you this way. It would frighten him." She didn't add that it had alarmed her to her bones. Senec gave a shallow sigh and she felt more than saw that he had closed his eyes again.

But she knew him, knew his strength and tenacity. He had asked for his son, asked for his posterity, and he would fight his way back. A warlord had no choice.

* * * *

It was a family reunion of sorts, though no one knew how long it would last. Clearly, Senec could go nowhere. Caln, alerted by messenger that his brother lay grievously injured at Shembel, could go nowhere because it had started to snow heavily. Kaleel and his men, more accustomed to cold and snow, could have gone somewhere but the question was where.

They discussed it with Pytor's help in Senec's chamber, when he was well enough to sit up in bed and take nourishment. Just as she had learned the plans of men while sitting in Atulfa's red tent, now she learned them in Westenian chambers loaned to them.

"The priests will seize power," Senec was observing, "if I cannot get back. They will choose another, probably Torm of Twin Rocks, and take it through him."

"You sent them enough tribute to keep them loyal for a time," Kaleel said.

Ifelsten also shook his head. "Caln has no reverence for your priests. If I send him down there with my men, you will have no more priests. It is the end of the problem."

"That is a point." Senec did not sound as if the thought bothered him despite the fact that a priest was translating for him. Granted that Pytor was not of the Covetian priesthood, he had survived the slaughter of his own when Covetians overran Westenia, and Ganina winced for him.

"My father gave them too much power," Senec added. "He was pious. It was difficult to dissuade him."

No, Ganina thought, Atulfa who was pious appeased the priests while his son, who was not, would not. But it could be dangerous.

"Well, I may have Juragians over my border," Kaleel argued, "if I do not soon return."

Ganina had avoided her father largely by never being where he was, but this time she could not avoid it. Possibly she would not be able to avoid it in the future, either. Inexplicably as she saw it, Kaleel and Senec seemed to have formed a liking and trust for one another. It made sense in a way. Her father had worried time out of mind about the Juragians. They bordered his section of Covetia and had lightning fire the Covetians lacked. He had married her into Atulfa's tribe to form a buffer in one direction, but it was the other border that really concerned him.

If he had wanted power in the south, she thought he would have left Senec at the bottom of the cliff and taken it. His forces far exceeded whatever the priests could conjure, given that Atulfa's tribe and the tribes of the fathers all were gone. But he hadn't done it. Clearly wary of spreading his forces too thin, he planned to leave that portion to Senec, now married to his daughter. That had played right into his hands and explained why he had not objected to their marriage, viewed as improper by some. He had always been a good tactician, just not a good husband or father.

"We will work it out," Ifelsten decided. He was only their host and could not dissuade anyone from leaving, but it made no sense. All their men and horses were worn from battle and the weather was settling in foul. The only ones who could move were the southern Covetians and they were depleted in number, no matter how much trouble the priests might foment.

"Just rest," Kaleel said, rising and pausing briefly to put a hand on Senec's shoulder. Ganina stared at him, frankly amazed. Was the old warrior going soft? She could not believe it.

He wasn't. Giving her a direct, challenging stare he said—in front of everyone—"Do you intend speaking to me again, daughter?"

"No," she shot back. She could not see the two of them, profiles similar, locked in a death stare—only the reaction of those who could. It was Senec who broke the stalemate.

"What is your complaint?" he asked her. "Your father made what marriage for you he could and now you have a better one. It is not that I am ungrateful for your care, but show some respect."

She flushed hot and cold. For days she had nursed him, never leaving his side except to check on Gilya, and now he took her father's part. She felt the break of that linkage even more acutely than she did her father's behavior and it made her angry, and incautious.

"I give it where it is due," she responded, then flinched reflexively as Ifelsten inserted himself quickly between her and Kaleel. She realized her father had been about to clout her and it would not have been the first time, but Ifelsten had blocked him.

"This will gain us nothing," he said.

Kaleel spit on the expensive rug. "She is not worth it, I warn you." With a grunt of disgust, he turned and walked through the doorway.

Her father's double meaning was clear. Still hot and cold and too much aware of Senec's eyes on her, Ganina muttered something nonsensical and left as well, but Pytor nodded courteously to her husband and followed with some alacrity.

"Ganina," he called and she halted, turning back to him. He was a priest, after all. No matter how angry she was, she could not ignore him. Uncharacteristically, he laid hands on her to turn her into a corner. There were too many eyes observing them in the open hall.

"Do not cost Ifelsten his life for your pride," he said.

So their gentle priest had teeth. Ganina gave him an insolent look but did not speak because she couldn't think of a thing to say.

"He did only what your husband could not do," Pytor warned. "Do not make more of it than that. He will not."

Left with nowhere else to go, Ganina spun on her heel and, reluctantly, went back to her own quarters. No one was there but Senec, still sitting up. Her looked at her quizzically as she came in, closing the door.

"I do not understand you, Ganina," he said. "Your father has been a loyal ally."

"Is that all that matters?" she asked, but she was afraid she already knew the answer. "He has been as nothing to me, all my life, Senec. He threw me to your people like a bone to be chewed. You know it. You know what they did to me."

Her husband just shrugged. "That was the women. No man knows what they will do."

Chapter Nineteen

Ganina brooded for days, her state of mind not helped by the fact that sleet and snow kept most people inside. Her only relief was to take Gilya to play in the snow or to visit the black pony. He had been ecstatic to be reunited with the pony that he remembered and she could see his father's love of horses etched in the child. For that matter, she saw his father stamped entirely on him. It was the call of blood, she supposed. He still liked his friend Ifelsten and his toy horses, but he had not forgotten Senec—not for an instant. She did not attempt to dissuade him from spending hours with his father while he healed; a boy needed a father. But she preferred to spend her time elsewhere.

Senec said nothing. He didn't seem to mind. The only way she knew of his displeasure was his remark when he met with the other men that they did not need her tantrums, and he threw her out. After that she slept in the dressing room with Gilya, but her husband did not seem to mind that either. In short, he paid no attention to her.

When she couldn't stand it any more, she climbed in bed with him in the middle of the night.

He stirred. "Have you finished?"

"Finished what?"

"Being angry."

"Probably not," she replied. "But I have missed you."

He turned, much more easily than he had done in weeks. "Then show me."

"How?" She didn't think even Senec could make love with his bones broken a short time before. But she had underestimated him.

"This way." With one hand he lifted her leg over his hip, with the other moved her against his ready arousal. Feeling his hand firmly planted on her backside, she made a sound of pure, unbridled lust and pushed herself onto him. He made love to her for hours, expending himself and then resting, only to wake and start all over again. It was a glut of sex not ending until the dawn, when she slept, exhausted, hands curled against his chest. His will had broken hers and they both knew it.

* * * *

It did not surprise her, after that, when Senec pronounced himself ready to travel. She was only astonished by where.

The horses were lined up in front of the hall, hooves stamping and bits jingling, before she knew, and then she realized why no one had told her. Then she realized why Senec had ridden past her with Gilya on the front of his horse. It was not purely fatherly affection. Gilya was bait, making sure that she would follow.

Ifelsten, who had seemed curiously remote since defending her, bid them farewell with a simple hand to her knee—kindly, not overly familiar.

"Be careful in those mountains," he said. "Slippery up there this time of year."

She stared at Senec's back, disappearing ahead of her in the line of riders and pack animals. Mountains? There was only one place they could be going that there were mountains. Northern Covetia. Her's father's kingdom. Senec was taking her home.

She was so dumbfounded that she must have ridden two miles before her brain began to function. If he had wanted to send her home, he would have simply taken his men and departed for the lowlands, leaving her to the tender mercies of the father who had never shown her any. He hadn't done that, so this had some tactical advantage she couldn't see. Whether or not he would leave her up there in the mountains, of course, she had no idea. She rode along, numb and dead to the world.

It was still snow-covered but less than it had been, a brief thaw having melted much of the snow. There was some heat in the sun and occasional rills of water ran in little rivulets, preparing for spring, but she was not deceived. This was low land compared to the mountain passes. They would have trouble there if they were not careful. She knew that land; Senec did not. She wondered what her father could have said to convince him to make the trip. But Senec's few men and her father's more numerous troops rode together, seemingly bonded by their recent killing spree, while she rode with the pack animals.

At the first rest stop, her husband seemed to think she had been sufficiently humiliated. Sulking atop a log from which someone had at least cleared the snow for her, she glanced at the chest of his war horse as it drew up to her. Senec swung down and offered her a drinking flask. It was watered wine and she drank gladly. Dropping his horse's rein, he sank down in a crouch alongside her.

"You could ride with us, you know," he told her, "if you can bear your father's company."

"Where are we going?" she asked.

"To his camp. Caln and Ifelsten have agreed to hold the border for us. In the meantime, I will go north, visiting the border lords as we go. Some have hinted rather broadly to your father that they would come back south with us. They have not been faring well and I will give them the lands of the tribes of memory in exchange for their service. I will return your father's men to their own camp and come south again, picking up those who wish to join me as I go."

It was a masterful stroke if he could control those men, Ganina thought. Then again, had he not just demonstrated how easily he could control her? He was a skillful manipulator. It would have been so much easier if she had not wanted him, but looking at him—beard neatly trimmed, hazel eyes crinkled with something that might have been humor, seemingly carefree in the burgeoning early spring day—she could not deny that she did. He was much better, seemingly restored to health, the epitome of vitality. She didn't understand how he did it.

"I will not be seen to leave your father, Ganina," he said when she didn't answer at once. "We must present a united front to the men. And Gilya is enjoying his company."

"My father despises children," she said from long experience. "I would not leave your son with him if I were you."

"He wants a grandson, I think."

She got to her feet in a huff. "Well, so do I. You might try praying to those gods you dislike."

"Nonsense." He got up easily, taking his horse's reins and beginning to walk with her and her pony. She was heading for the front of the column, so he had won—again. "I will fuck you the length of Covetia. That's all that's needed."

She gave him a cool look. "It couldn't hurt to try, I suppose."

Chapter Twenty

It was reasonably pleasant at first. The sun remained out and they were warmly dressed and well provisioned, so they were comfortable. Ganina rode a crossbred pony given to her by Ifelstein, larger than their Covetian ponies but heavy-coated and surefooted like his mountain counterparts. She rode beside her husband and father, saying little to either of them, but taking Gilya in turn as they passed him back and forth like a parcel. Covetian boys rode very young, but it was too long a ride for him to make on his small pony.

Senec seemed at pains to keep his word. As soon as they had camped and dinner was done, he took her hand to lead her to their tent, followed by her father's sour look. Senec wasn't even attempting to hide the fact that he would bed his wife in full view of the camp. Ganina felt her cheeks burning, but she followed him obediently and received her reward in minutes, pinned beneath him. One pull at her bodice, baring her breasts, followed by one tug at his trousers, lowering them, and he took her before she had time to breathe. Breathing was not necessary, in any case, she told herself. She felt like a receptacle, but after all that's what she was. He wanted a child. She was the means to get one. She sensed it was only the first of what would be many such nights and, for the first time, was less than welcoming.

Winter had held harder to the greater heights. She was not sorry to see the first border camp looming against the bulk of mountains they would soon have to cross. She saw at once that it was a poor camp with scrawny ponies and milling sheep, but there was welcome peat smoke from various chimneys and round tents of densely woven felt that promised warm shelter. Apparently, her father's men had been at work establishing contact, because outriders with spears carried in stirrup holders met them while they were still some distance from the camp and rode in with them. They were expected and would receive what hospitality such a poor chieftain could provide, but people like this were tough, uncompromising tribesmen and very clannish. It was all that ensured their survival. They would be wary of outsiders and probably hard to win over.

Accompanied now also by yapping dogs and trailing children, they rode to the head tent. Carrying Gilya before her, Ganina reined back slightly so as not to present herself with the men. Her turn would come, the more so if she carried a child, but until such time as she was acknowledged, she did not exist. She had returned to her father's lands, or close enough. This would be the pattern of their visits: cautious welcome from people who shared her language but not much else, a day or two of hunting for the men and boredom for the women, nightly counsels of which she would learn virtually nothing and an obligatory feast before leaving.

She never knew precisely what took place in that camp or in the next several camps. Senec was non-committal, simply saying he had made offers and would revisit them on his way south to see who had decided to accompany him. She did not think he had been foolish enough to bribe anyone. Caln's gold and the tribute from Sowetia could not last indefinitely. These men would come for land or not at all and they would have to come with the consent of their chieftains or hard feelings would be engendered. Most of them lived by scavenging and herding, preying on travelers and raids into Juragia and Westenia. They could pose no real threat to more organized camps. All the same, their little bites could sting.

Moreover, from what scraps she did obtain, Ganina became convinced her father and Senec envisioned carving Covetia into two allied parts, north and south, to guard against a newly-powerful Westenia. If they had their way, there would be no more place for the border campus. Kaleel's method would have been to obliterate them, but Ganina had already learned her husband did not destroy without purpose. If he could incorporate those tribes peacefully, he would do it.

Finally, there was only one left, lying at the very base of the mountains. She had been there a time or two as a child and knew her father still maintained closer ties with their chieftain than with the others. There was not exactly friendship between them, but they had done business at times and Kaleel found them useful in keeping Juragians off his lands. It should be a relatively pleasant visit.

* * * *

The last negotiations were the hardest, Senec had to admit. The camp of Trelgar was not as penurious as those that lay closer to the plain. Here there were waters to carry furs downriver for trade and return with goods other camps lacked, perhaps even the prized crossbows he had not yet obtained for his own camp. The people were expert bowmen…and women. He was surprised to learn that Trelgar's wife and three daughters were archers every bit as competent as the men.

"Do you prefer foot or horseback?" Trelgar asked, pulling out an obviously well loved and burnished bow behind the main building where his family resided and where the two of them conferred. There was no shortage of timber and at last Senec had escaped the omnipresent tents of other encampments. It gave the camp a strong, clean smell of cedar. He judged it might well be a healthier place, too, less prone to fever. He liked it, feeling more comfortable there than at the squalid camps below this one. Ganina seemed happier as well, despite her stated disdain for her father's lands. Perhaps she could find some peace there, he thought—possibly even enough to give him the child he now conceded he must have. If his plan succeeded, Gilya would not be enough. He needed more sons.

"On horse," he replied matter-of-factly. His lands were plain and steppe for the most part. "But archers of your sort would be more than welcome. We have good and fertile land. All it needs is water and men to work it."

"I don't know." Trelgar nocked an arrow, then let it fall again as if changing his mind. "My men are not much for digging. There is one archer, though…I would like you to see. This one might be of interest."

The archer of interest rounded the corner of the building at Trelgar's call and Senec suppressed a smile, understanding at once why he had been accorded the honor of a private meeting with the tribal leader. This chieftain who knew his father-in-law was not even being subtle. Trelgar wanted an alliance without losing any of his men. A woman, on the other hand…well, that might be possible.

"My daughter," he introduced the tall, lissome girl. "This is Astera. She is our middle jewel."

A middle child, neither the expected first nor the favored youngest. This one was a bargaining chip, but jewel was not too strong a descriptor. Senec viewed her with total respect. She was not beautiful as Ganina was…she was a warrior. Tall, dark haired with a striking profile under strong brows…feminine, but the gods, she was impressive. Soft deerskin clung to every curve while boots that reached above the knee accentuated her length of leg. Her smile was surprisingly warm and gracious…she was a goddess who could be thawed, that smile said…and in no way obsequious. She was looking at him every bit as boldly as he was at her. This was not a compliant creature with Ganina's sweetness. Astera was a woman to bed if he could, but she would not be easy.

"You two are young," Trelgar dismissed himself. "Go and shoot for pleasure if you like. I have had enough for one day."

"It is a glorious day for pleasure," Astera agreed. She carried two bows, one over each shoulder. "Will you come?"

Chapter Twenty-One

They were amazingly kind to her at Trelgar's camp. Ganina didn't know if it was because their leader remembered her as a little girl, but in any case, she was enjoying herself. The feast their night before leaving was sumptuous—roe deer, pig and venison roasting on spits—wild turnips and berries, bread and mead and beer, everything the camp could provide. With no shortage of firewood, they were warm and more than merry.

Comfortably cushioned on deerskins and furs, more than a little tipsy from spirits offered without measure, she was feeling almost sorry to leave on the morrow.

"May I sit?" a girl asked politely. Ganina looked up with a smile. Yes, she remembered this one—it was Trelgar's middle daughter. A very handsome girl, seemingly friendly. So Ganina willingly made a space for her.

Astera simply folded her legs to sit. She held herself like the demi-goddess she resembled, Ganina thought. But she did not put on airs, passing bread and wine to Ganina without hesitation, serving a guest.

"You like them?" she asked, gesturing to dancers in front of them. Perhaps a dozen of the tribe's girls, dressed in intricately beaded clothing and head coverings, had danced in impressive unison for their visitors, stepping en masse over decorated poles they used for a ritual dance to the accompaniment of wild music. Ganina was wishing every camp could have been like this one.

"Very much," she replied. "They are wonderful."

"It is good that you like our customs," Astera said, helping herself to wine. She paused briefly, wiping her mouth as the men did—on her tunic. Ganina smiled, reminded of Ifelsten.

"I have lain with your husband," Astera said without preamble. "He is good. Would you accept me as second wife?"

An earthquake could not have shaken her more. Ganina felt the blood drain from her face.

Astera was simply looking at her—questioningly. "I do not wish to consign myself to a life of misery with a jealous first wife," she explained, as if explanation was the only thing needed. "I am young and can give him children. I would have no hard feelings with you."

Abruptly, it was all abundantly clear. Her father was behind this. He wanted grandchildren to cement his alliance with Senec, but in two years she had not provided any. This girl was not blood, but he had close ties with her father. She would do in Ganina's place and apparently Senec was in agreement or he would not have been with her. They had been kind to her in Trelgar's camp because they pitied her.

She was useless. He was done with her. It accounted for his lack of respect, taking her to his tent in full view of the camp and using her as he had done, without tenderness. He had tried his best to get her with child, as he had promised, and when that failed, he had been offered this girl…and accepted.

She was dust. Without a word, she got up and walked out of the building. No one came after her.

* * * *

From across the room where Senec sat, drinking with the other men, he saw the entrance of his prospective wife and the departure of his present one. It was not what he had anticipated, but then this entire visit was not going according to plan. Perhaps it was going better.

Astera was everything he had expected, and more. An afternoon of shooting for both sport and pleasure had turned into one of pleasure alone. As sunset drew near, when cold would have rendered the process uncomfortable, he had taken her down, laughing and contesting with him, on a bed of bracken. They had both known what he was about. He let her assault him sufficiently to satisfy her honor and when he had remained undeterred, she opened her legs. In her tribal culture she was well within her rights to resist until he proved he was man enough to have her. If she had continued fighting, he could not have taken her without provoking a feud. But once assured that he would be suitable, she gave herself to him without reservation despite the unmistakable proof that she had not done it before, showing no sign of pain or fear. She would be suitable as well.

They were as good as wed. All that remained was to establish a dowry with her father and it would be favorable to Senec or Trelgar would never have sent her. Now she had said or done something that had caused Ganina to leave the building with a thunderstruck expression. Perhaps conversation was not Astera's best gift, he thought.

But her father had another one in mind.

"Did you find my daughter to your liking?" Trelgar inquired pleasantly, and pointedly.

"Very much so," Senec replied. Had the girl been a disaster he could have refused, but she had done exactly what she was supposed to do, with obvious enjoyment. There was no fault in her and Senec realized with a certain sense of guilt that he had found her response more gratifying than Ganina's tepid one of late. He had been faithful to Ganina for over two years, more than most men would have done. His previous reluctance to take on a second wife was diminishing rapidly, especially with Trelgar's next words.

"Her dowry is fifty crossbows," Astera's father told him.

"Indeed." Not by a single inflection did Senec acknowledge what a generous offer this was...no, more than generous. A dowry like that could literally keep his people alive and allow them to flourish. He did not need men from Trelgar if he had fifty crossbows. But he saw now that he did need his daughter.

"It is settled, then," he agreed. In his heart he acknowledged a pang for Ganina, whom he knew would not take it well. He owed her greatly for the life of his son and the care she had given him after his injury. It was why he had never abandoned her and never would. She would not demand to return to her father; she hated him. That left her as he had found her, essentially a camp hanger-on. It was a cruel fate, but what had befallen his people was even worse. He could not risk anything like that again.

Chapter Twenty-Two

She was damned if she would attend the wedding festivities. Ganina had not been one warlord's daughter and another's wife for nothing. She had faced worse odds running for her life from the tribes of the fathers. In the dark of night and the absence of witnesses, because everyone was in the main hall, she assembled a pack somewhat more fully equipped than the one Donleth had made for her. She would be going further this time. When it was finished, she went to the pony line and bridled the pony Ifelsten had given her and led him away. She did not take time to saddle him; no Covetian really needed a saddle. When she was sure they would not be overheard, she swung up onto him with her pack lashed to her back, clucked and left the camp, heading south.

Heavy snow lay above her, closer to the timberline. There would only be tatters of it, going south towards the spring thaw. The stars were clear, she knew the way and if she did not, the pony did. He would take her unerringly back to the stables where he had been raised, back to Ifelsten. If he did not want her, she would continue riding south, back to where the rest of Senec's tribe had perished, and add her bones to theirs.

This time she did not have Gilya to slow her progress, and

the gods only knew how much she missed him. His needs were the only thing that had given her pause, but even that had not been enough to stop her. He would be losing yet another mother and it would be hard, but he had been growing closer to Senec with every passing week. No matter the character of the second wife, and that she could not predict, Gilya was his father's first son and would always be safe. She could do no more for him, but he had been in effect her only child—the only one she could ever expect to have, now—and her heart ached with an actual physical pain.

No matter. Nothing mattered any more. She would have a head start of several hours, in the event anyone wanted to pursue her. They might actually be relieved, she thought, and leave her in peace. That was all she wanted.

* * * *

"I was very respectful," Astera defended herself. "I simply asked her if she would accept me as second wife."

"I think that she did not." Senec's tone was short-tempered.

"Where will she have gone?" Trelgar's voice held a note of real concern despite the awkwardness of Ganina's disappearance. He had known her since she was small and he was the father of daughters.

"My guess would be back to Shembel. They hosted her there the entire time we were in Sowetia. If she finds no welcome there, the Camp of the Horsetails is to the south. What is left of it, anyway."

"But she knows you'll be coming there," Kaleel pointed out.

Senec's expression was grim. "In that case she will seek death."

Everyone present was silent until Kaleel made a sound of irritation. "Then let her go to her fate. She has chosen."

Senec shook his head. "I cannot. I owe her for the life of my son. You do not repay such a debt with death."

No one could argue with that. He could not argue with it himself, although he knew there was more...much more. Senec had loved two people in his life—his mother and Caln. His mother was of memory and Caln was in Westenia, married to a Westenian woman and apparently intent on breeding up a whole pack of Westenian children. It was possible that their countries would be at war again one day and if they could not contrive to avoid each other on the field of battle as they had done before, it was conceivable that he would have to kill his own brother. Or Caln, who was fully able, would kill him.

It was dangerous to feel what he did for Ganina, but he could not lose her, too. His gentle wife, who had nevertheless survived a ride for her life that many men could not have done, had made up her mind to fight. If her only means was to run, well, sometimes that was all a woman could do. But he doubted she would be so lucky twice. There were dangers in the wastelands she didn't even understand.

"Then what will you do?" Astera asked.

Senec sighed deeply. "Go after her. She cannot be that many hours ahead. I'll bring her back kicking and screaming if I must. But I will not leave her to die."

"I will have horses brought," Kaleel said, but Senec shook his head.

"It will not be a long trip." He did not want witnesses to whatever might happen. There would be enough talk as it was. Nor did he want Ganina's reaction to the sight of her father. She could not be in her right mind, to have attempted to return to Shembel alone. It was suicide. "I will do this thing myself."

Kaleel opened his mouth to speak, but Senec cut him off as he had never done. "Do you think I cannot do it alone?"

What transpired between husband and wife was commonly conceded to be no one else's business. The older man backed down in the face of his challenge. "No."

"Then have my horse brought, and a pack. I should be back in a day, maybe two." His look softened as it fell on Astera. He didn't want to hurt her. But he had to acknowledge what he felt for Astera was the pride of conquest and a need for armament. "It will give you more time to plan. Nothing has changed except that I have a mad wife."

She snorted indelicately. "You already did."

* * * *

In truth, Ganina began to question her own sanity after her water ran out. For a time, she was able to locate brackish streams, enough for herself and the pony, but then there were no more. She was coming to some of the most arid lands they had crossed.

She began letting the pony go on a loose rein, scenting for water. There were water holes and he could find them better than she could. Finally he did, and she dismounted wearily, trailing his rein. He was well trained and would not leave her. There was no bucket at the hole, but there were wild gourds growing near the water source. Drawing a knife from her pack, she painstakingly cut the top from one, scooping what was inside with a stick and offering it to the pony. It was poor quality but he was hungry and ate it while she hacked at some vines. It was a job of work to pick them apart, but she did and twined them carefully, braiding them into three parts forming a net into which she placed the gourd. Thus turned into a vessel, it could be carefully lowered into the hole and bring up water. The shell would collapse eventually, but in the meantime, she could fill her water skins. It was a technique nomadic people had used time out of mind.

It was a slow process, though. First, she watered the pony, since her life depended on his. Only when he had drained the gourd many times did she drink. She was still drinking when he threw up his head and whinnied, looking back in the direction they had come.

Senec's piebald horse was easily distinguishable, his white patches seeming to glow in the rays of the sun behind him. Stupefied, she looked for additional riders but there were none. Her husband had come after her, alone. She thought she would rather have seen one of the mythical devils rumored to live in the wastelands. They would have been more welcome.

She could not outrun him. Her pony was smaller, and worn by travel and lack of adequate forage. She looked at the knife in her hand and wondered if she had the courage to use it, but she didn't. She wouldn't have minded using it on Senec at that moment, but already knew how futile such an effort would prove. He would laugh at her.

"So, you are alive," he observed, riding up. "I am surprised."

"The devil does not want me."

"Apparently." He dismounted, taking the gourd from her suddenly nerveless hand. The knife he ignored. "You got further than I thought you would. I'm out of water."

Competently and much faster than she had done, he repeated her motions in order to water his horse and then himself. He was dusty and suffering from a covering of horse hair, the same as she was, because it was spring and their horses were shedding. Without her leave, he dumped a gourd full of water over her head and then one over himself. She wondered why she had not thought of that.

"You could have saved yourself the trouble," she said. "I will not go back with you."

He shook himself like a dog, spraying her. "And how do you propose to stop me?"

"Go back to your whore."

"She is not a whore. She has a dowry of fifty crossbows. Do you know what that can do for our people?"

That stopped her for a moment. She had thought it was only lust that drove him, but then she chastised herself. Senec might lust after a woman, but he was driven by thought. The girl was handsome, but she could have worn a bag over her head if she brought fifty crossbows.

"Well, take her and welcome. I only wish to go south."

"To what?"

"To Shembel, or further if need be. Let me go, Senec. You have what you want."

The horses were eating the gourds. Taking a knife from his belt, he bent to hack off a couple of them and some vines before they were gone. Those might be useful. Then he looked up at her.

"Ifelsten has even more need of heirs than I do. He will not take a barren Covetian woman."

She shrugged. "Then I will go to the camp."

"There is nothing left but spirits. Do you wish to join them?"

Did she? The spirits of Donleth and Aben the pony boy, both of whom had saved her life, were there. Such spirits were good company on the journey. "What if I do?"

"Don't be stupid. Astera is a decent girl and you may yet have children. I have plenty for both of you."

Well, that she did not doubt, at least. "And you think I would lie with you when you have been with her?"

"Yes."

She was afraid of it, too, and all the more infuriated because he knew it. He was like a sweet poison for her, she thought in exasperation. She was likely to partake even if it killed her, and it would kill her pride to share him.

Unexpectedly, he stood up and put out a hand to cup the side of her face. She had expected anger but not gentleness and it disarmed her. She froze in indecision.

"You know this is a common arrangement," he said, reasonably. "No one will think less of you. She will keep to her place."

"In your bed?" He was still touching her and she threw off his hand like it was burning.

"Of course, in my bed. Did you think there would not be room for you?"

Chapter Twenty-Three

"Pah!" She spat in the soil, something her father would have done. He simply put both hands around her waist, holding her fast.

"What's really wrong, Nina? Are you afraid that I don't love you?"

His use of the nickname Gilya had given her was what finally broke her. She would have collapsed, sobbing, except that he held her up and against him. He wrapped his arms around her and held her while she buried her face against him, sobbing. She was crying for the abuse her father had heaped on her all her life…for the torment of the little wives…for the terror of her flight to Shembel…for the hollowness of having no child…sobbing out of fear and grief and things she could not even name.

He might have beaten her bloody. She had half expected him to. Instead, he held her and asked if she was afraid he didn't love her. Of course, it was exactly what she feared.

"You don't love me," she protested. "You don't love anybody. You don't dare."

She felt him flinch. They had hit each other as unerringly as any arrow.

"You're wrong," he said quietly.

Gently, he bent his head to kiss her face, tears and all. With his thumbs, he traced her tear tracks, framing her face in his hands. He kissed her forehead, her neck, the top of her shoulder while she held to him, just feeling his breath and the beat of his heart. She tangled her hands in the cloth of his tunic, clinging to him as he unlaced hers, kissing the cleft between her breasts. She made a wordless sound of passion, telling him that he had reached her, and leaned back over his hands, letting him support her as he kissed a line inside her tunic. Working one hand free, she pulled it awkwardly over her head and stood against him, naked to the waist. There was no one anywhere for miles. They were utterly alone except for the wind and the quiet sounds of the horses foraging. He pulled off his tunic as well and they stood simply pressed together, feeling each other. It was the oldest message the world contained.

"You must trust me—trust me to do what is right," he said. "Can you do that?"

"Yes," she finally answered, and he unlaced her trousers and then his own, pushing them down. With one hand he followed an unerring path down her body, welcome and familiar. It had been long since he had caressed her that way, simply for her pleasure. She sucked in her breath as he reached the coppery curls at the juncture of her thighs, threading his fingers through and rubbing gently just where he knew she liked it while his other hand pressed her buttocks, moving her against it. She could feel her legs trembling.

She couldn't wait for him any longer.

"Put me down," she said, struggling to kick out of her trousers and her boots. With an arm behind her neck and another beneath her thighs, he simply scooped her and lowered her onto the wreck of their clothes, kneeling inside her legs. She expected him to take her at once, as urgently as she wanted him, but he didn't. Instead he grasped her chin gently, forcing her to look at him.

"No one will ever love you the way I do," he said.

She circled him with her arms, drawing down on him, and threw her head back wantonly as he thrust inside her, already locked into the familiar rhythm she knew so well. Yet it was indisputably, miraculously different, better and more than it had ever been, because he loved her.

* * * *

She had wondered, fearfully, how she would be met upon her return to Trelgar's camp, but it seemed totally unchanged. There were no visible preparations for any festivities and no one spoke, just watching silently as the chieftain from the south rode through their encampment with his runaway wife.

Senec stopped in front of the main building where Trelgar and his family lived, where an alert pony boy took their mounts although he, too, was silent. Ganina, grimy and expecting the worst, followed a step behind him into the building. Presumably in disgrace, she would demonstrate her assumption of place. But that, she thought, was all she would do.

Trelgar knew they were there. He met them in the hallway where everyone magically seemed to melt away.

"My daughter no longer wishes to marry you," he told Senec. "We should talk."

Talk was good, compared with what he might have done. "Go with the women," he instructed Ganina, gesturing to where Astera and her mother were now coming down the empty hall. Without a further word, he and Senec moved through an inside door much like the ones Ganina had seen at Shembel, but she hardly noticed them leaving. To her utter consternation, Astera's mother held Gilya by the hand. Seeing her, he shrieked and raced at top speed down the long wooden corridor and into her arms.

"Oh, Gilya," she murmured, clutching him to her, inhaling his little boy scent.

"Mama, Mama," he cried. She could have sworn she felt her heart break in two. "Where did you go?"

It was the mother, Dracina, who answered. "She went for a long ride, Gilya, but Papa brought her back." She looked at Ganina over his head as the child climbed her like a tree, arms around her neck, holding on for dear life. "She will not go away again."

Ganina shook her head. "I am not—" she began, but the

woman cut her off.

"You *are* his mother," she said firmly. "He has no other. Shame on you to have left him. My daughter can get another husband. But this child has only you."

Chastened to the point of speechlessness, Ganina got up, lifting Gilya onto her hip although he was getting too big for it.

"Now let us have tea," Dracina relented. "You look wretched."

Inside a small chamber mercifully strewn with pillows, because Ganina was more saddle sore than she had ever been in her life, they took tea from a silent serving woman. Gilya—worn out from emotion and probably, Ganina thought, from grieving— curled in her lap, thumb in his mouth. He had not done that in a long time. She stroked his hair, overcome.

"So," Astera said, "you would rather die in the wastelands than share with me. I told you I would not suffer a bitter first wife all my life, and I will not suffer you. Your husband has taken my honor, but I was willing. I already know there will be no child from what we did. So…" She popped a teacake into her mouth, apparently not too offended to eat. "My father will ask recompense and it will not be cheap. There will be no dowry, and you will go."

Ganina was impressed. Young as she was, this girl had taken charge, disdainful and never losing dignity while her mother sat by without a word. Dracina had said what she meant to say.

"You would have made a good second wife," Ganina conceded, "but you are right. Senec is mine. I will not let him go."

"Did he beat you?" Astera inquired.

"No."

"Too bad." The girl shrugged. "Well, that is his affair. But you will get nothing from us."

She and Senec were equally in disgrace now. He had cost the tribe their lives and she had cost them the crossbows that might have saved them.

"We will be gone in the morning, if my Lord agrees," she said.

Chapter Twenty-Four

In the morning, Senec informed her of a change in plans. They had lost time due to her escapade and would not be proceeding to her father's camp. Instead, their two forces would part at the outskirts of Trelgar's camp, with Kaleel's men heading north and Senec's south. No one had to tell her that Kaleel and Senec had probably argued over her, and that Senec had remained adamant. His number would be greatly reduced. But she doubted they had broken their agreement entirely and Senec anticipated adding men as they went south, back to the Camp of the Horsetails.

Ganina was not sorry. She thought the only one sorry to see Kaleel go was Gilya, who seemed attached to him. Perhaps if she had been a boy, her father might have loved her. As a daughter, he had no use for her. There was only one person who loved her—well, one adult, anyway—even if he referred to it only obliquely. She was Senec's wife and it was all that mattered now.

He also advised her they would not be stopping at Shembel and she just smiled. Her husband had lain with another woman. There was no getting around that. But she had nearly done the same thing with the man who had been his enemy. She thought if Ifelsten had not held to the edge of his reserve she would have gone to him, probably with disastrous results.

* * * *

They went back through the lower camps, but when Senec packed at sunrise as they prepared to leave the last one, on their final push to the south, she was speechless. Within the privacy of their tent, rewrapping things for travel, he drew out the unmistakable shape of a crossbow.

"Just one," he explained. "Caln's gold bought us one crossbow, but it's enough. All our weapons makers rode with me to Sowetia." He nodded toward the tent flap. "They are right outside."

Yes, those men had remained loyal to Senec through everything, just as she had. Tested, tried, exasperated at times, fearful of his death but dogged and determined--all of them had stayed with him to give honor to their dead and raise their camp again.

Fascinated, she moved close beside him to run her hand wonderingly over the cool, smooth deadliness of the weapon. The other hand she held almost unconsciously curled around Senec's upper arm. This weapon was strength; it was survival—as he was hers.

"They can make these," he went on. "It will take time, it will not be as quick as bringing fifty bows with us, but it can be done. All we needed was a pattern."

"I knew you would do it," she said thoughtfully. "I wasn't sure how, but I knew."

"We have enough people now. A few women are coming, too," he said. "Most of them would not leave their men."

"I will not leave you again."

"I know."

It was time to tell him. They had been two months traveling down the length of Covetia and taking the dogleg needed to bypass Shembel. Her courses had not troubled her and, at first, she had thought it was due to the hardship of travel. But then she began to feel unwell and then her courses had not come again.

"I am with child."

Her reward was his slow smile, looking down at her. Others might find him inscrutable, but he was her husband and she knew when he was pleased.

"Well, I told you," he replied.

He could claim the credit and should. But she knew it was more than that. Loving on the good earth had produced the result that all their nights in warm tents and silken coverlets had not. She had a true child of Covetia in her womb. Son or daughter, it did not matter. This was something from the gods, powerful and destined.

"We will go slowly if you need to," he promised. "We have enough stores for some months. I will buy livestock from the camps that are still standing and the men can begin to turn the soil. We cannot plant this year, but we will get by until the spring, when we can. When will the baby come?"

"In the winter."

"A winter's child. Good." Embracing her with his free arm, he kissed her forehead.

Gilya would have a brother or sister. Perhaps, with luck, he would have more. Their camp would live again and Senec, unlike his father, was a man who could hold the peace. Or he could make war, if needful. But peace was better.

It was all she had ever wanted.

Senec stepped back to wrap the crossbow once more, adding it to his pack. He shouldered it carefully, lifting the tent flap.

"Come," he said. "The sun is rising."

THE END

About the Author

Fantasy poetry driven by myths and legends has been my passion for as long as I can remember. I was published in poetry before catching the romance writing bug. I bring that background to my writing along with a lifelong addiction to horses, an 18 year career in various areas of psychiatric social services and many trips to Ireland, where I nurture my muse. My published works range from contemporary fantasy romance to fantasy historical, futuristic, science fiction and historical romance. Currently I live in rural Pennsylvania with a "motley crew" of rescue animals. You can see my books at www.miriamnewman.com.

Blog: www.thecelticroseblog.blogspot.com
Facebook:
https://www.facebook.com/AuthorMiriamNewman/

Other books by Miriam Newman

Spirit Awakened

In a pre-medieval land recently torn by war, a woman with no voice and no memories struggles to survive. Drawn by need to a small farm, she encounters a man equally in need, though for different reasons. They are each other's only hope, and the future for their land. In a time of spiritual awakening, can they and their country survive? Or will the twin enemies of fear and persecution triumph?

The Chronicles of Alcinia

Available for the first time as an e-book bundle, the award-winning fantasy historical series The Chronicles of Alcinia weaves a tale of war, history, passion and romance. In Book I, The King's Daughter, Tarabenthia of Alcinia should grow to inherit her father's throne by the rocky cliffs of the sea. When invaders seize her land, what will she sacrifice in the name of love? In Book II, Heart of the Earth, the Northern Prince who has always wanted Tia saves her life. But will the price of his protection be too high? And finally in Book III, Ice Maiden, readers who wondered about the fate of Tia's oldest son have their answer. Sometimes heart-wrenching, always powerful, this is a tale of heroes and the women who love them.

Invanine

He was her slave in one land, her lover in another. When the king's sister saves a rebel from a troubled province, her act of mercy changes her life irrevocably and influences the course of her country's future.

The Eagle's Woman

Son of an impoverished, dying Norse chieftain, Ari raids for booty and slaves so he can feed his people. Pagan himself, still he spares priests though he sells them. He's a heathen, a murderer, and it is a sin for any Christian woman to love him. Yet when he abducts Maeve from her peaceful Irish fishing village, he may have found the one woman who can.

The Comet

An ambitious young Norman knight, Neel, is seriously wounded at the Battle of Hastings and nursed back to health by a Saxon girl, Rowena. For her, it is only a matter of Christian duty and she is shocked to receive his proposal of marriage in return. She dares not refuse, but how can she love a Norman?

Excerpt from Spirit Awakened

By Miriam Newman

The girl had forgotten her name. It was a fact so simple yet so profound that it was like the earth moving beneath her feet. Her belly was heavy with child, though the rest of her looked like parchment stretched over sticks. She could not remember when she had last eaten properly or even what proper food was.

She did remember that it was summer when the enemy invaded. There was a confused, swirling sense of being in a place she considered home and of faces appearing in windows where men had slit the membrane that kept out rain. She remembered screams and pain and the sensation of being raised bodily and thrown to the floor. Her head hit what must have been floorboards with a hollow, imploding sound like a gourd splitting. And then there was nothing.

She could not remember her name, or how to speak, or where to find her people. They were forgotten, too. She had forgotten her place in life. Now, there was only hunger, thirst, and the baby about to be born. She had very little time.

And very little water. She had trailed a line of hollowed containers behind her to take some back to the cave where she had wintered. When she heard their dim clatter on the rocks, she looked back in alarm. Though it was not yet time for the enemy's women to pass by on their way to the water hole, she could not risk making any noise. It was only that she had grown so clumsy. Dull, cramping pain gnawed at her, but she would not stop. There was dried meat at the cave, and moss and sinew and some cloth stolen from laundry lines. But she still needed water.

Inch by painstaking inch, she descended the sheer face of rock and gnarled tree roots which made passage to her cave unappealing and nearly impossible for a woman weighed down by pregnancy. The very difficulty of passage was her insurance against trespassers, but it worked against her, as well. She would lose some of her precious water on the way up, and much of her strength.

Her legs were shaking when she reached solid ground, but there was no time to spare. As quickly as her bulk permitted, she slid into concealing reeds and crouched, stock still, listening. Birdsong interrupted by her appearance resumed, sweet and chipper; she was alone. Carefully, she slipped to the edge of the water, waiting until flotsam dislodged by her advent settled. When the water was clear, she dipped her containers, one by one. She had been doing it for days, storing it at the cave, but she sensed her opportunities were coming to an end.

A curious and incautious fish appeared, attracted by movement. The girl knew he was a gift from the gods. Because he was, the fish only swam through her ankles as if they had been tree trunks. He permitted the infinitely slow, incremental looping of her hands beneath him…the almost imperceptible elevation of her palms that cupped him, surely and lethally…and the brutally quick toss onto the bank that ensured a meal. That fish was the difference between life and death, so the wild girl forced herself to snatch his slimy, wriggly silver-blueness by a desperately thrashing tail. She smacked his head solidly onto rock. Now, she and the fish had been treated similarly, except he was dead and she was not.

DCL Publications, LLC

www.thedarkcastlelords.net

Find our books at any fine online retailer.